Chasing the Cl
by Lucy F

Text Copyright 2019 © Lucy Felthouse.

All Rights Reserved.

With the exception of quotes used in reviews, this book may not be reproduced or used in whole or in part by any means existing without written permission from the aforementioned author.

Warning: The unauthorised reproduction or distribution of this copyrighted work is illegal. No part of this book may be scanned, uploaded or distributed via the Internet or any other means, electronic or print, without the author's written permission.

This book is a work of fiction and any resemblance to persons, living or dead, is purely coincidental. The characters are productions of the author's imagination and used fictitiously.

To Charles,

Happy reading!

L Felthouse

Table of Contents

Prologue

Chapter One

Chapter Two

Chapter Three

Chapter Four

Chapter Five

Chapter Six

Chapter Seven

Chapter Eight

Chapter Nine

Chapter Ten

Chapter Eleven

Chapter Twelve

Chapter Thirteen

Chapter Fourteen

About the Author

If You Enjoyed Chasing the Chambermaid

Prologue

Only the slop, slop, slopping sound of her painfully slow footsteps through the thick, sucking mud convinced Connie White she was actually making any progress. Her limbs and extremities had long since gone so numb that she couldn't be sure otherwise.

Come on, Con, just a little bit further. That sign said something about an estate, and an estate means buildings. A bloody cowshed will do—anything for some respite from this infernal sodding weather.

She pushed on for several more minutes, then gasped with shock and relief when her next step met not with sloppy mud or waterlogged grass, but a track. A rough track, but a track nonetheless. And it had to lead somewhere, surely? It ran left to right across the line she'd been taking, so Connie had to make a decision. Which way would lead her to… something? She was already soaked to the skin and freezing cold, so a couple of seconds of rumination wouldn't make the slightest bit of difference to her physical state. She *really* didn't want to end up going in the wrong direction and heading further away from any semblance of civilisation.

She took a breath and remembered her gran's—long since dead, bless her—nonsensical motto—or one of them, anyway: *If in doubt, turn left.*

Connie shrugged, and another of her gran's daft phrases flitted into her brain. *In for a penny, in for a pound.*

She hoiked her backpack higher, hunched her shoulders against the relentless wind and rain, and turned left. Moments later, she was rewarded as the hulking shape of a building appeared from the sheets of wind-buffeted rain. Excitement gave her a burst of energy, spurring her on. Fifty feet. Forty. Twenty-five. God, what *was* this place? It looked so old and decrepit the Vikings could have left it behind. *Doesn't matter. If it provides even a modicum of shelter, it's an improvement on where you slept last night.* The wooden bench on the tiny village's green hadn't exactly been the warmest or most comfortable place to lay her head. And she shuddered to think about what would have happened if someone unsavoury had happened across her, alone and vulnerable. She'd been very glad to wake up and hurriedly continue on her journey that morning.

The last few feet went by in a blur of motion, her body still numb and not entirely under her control. At least the track was easier to walk on. It wasn't particularly smooth, but at least it wasn't trying to pull off her walking boots, like the sucking mud had been.

Finally, she burst through the building's heavy door, only the adrenaline pumping in her veins making it possible to even shift the thing. *Fuck, I'm exhausted.*

The last thing she remembered was shucking off her backpack and slamming the door against the elements. Then silence.

Chapter One

"Oh, look—I think she's waking up. Thank the Lord."

Connie frowned as the unfamiliar female voice reached her ears, then she cracked her eyes open, squinting against the light. She quickly came to the conclusion it wasn't just the voice that was unfamiliar. The bed she lay in was unfamiliar, the room was unfamiliar, and she didn't have the foggiest idea who the two people gazing concernedly at her were. She blinked. Nope—still the same. Still didn't have a clue. Aware it was the cheesiest of clichés, she asked, "Where am I? And who are you?"

An attractive, red-haired woman Connie guessed to be in her late forties, maybe early fifties, and dressed in smart business attire gave a gentle smile and shuffled her chair a little closer to the bed. "Hello. Welcome back to the land of the living. You've had us very worried. You're in the staff quarters of my hotel—I own and run Bowdley Hall Hotel. I'm Frances McKenzie. This," she waved towards the man on the other side of the bed, who was probably ten years her junior and a couple of years older than Connie, "is my estate gardener, Will MacIntyre. He found you in the outbuilding."

As Connie's brain absorbed the words, spoken in a soft, lilting accent, something tickled at the edges of her consciousness. Something she ought to know, but couldn't… quite… place.

As she struggled to a sitting position, her brain seemed to click into gear. Of course, she was in Scotland! It all came back to her—leaving *him,* ditching anything that could identify her, and scarpering for the wilderness of the Scottish Highlands with only the clothes on her back and as many possessions as she could cram into her rucksack. What she hadn't betted on—and she should have known better, really, since this was *Scotland,* for heaven's sake— was the weather. A pleasant, sun-bathed hike, almost pleasant enough to make her forget what she was running from in the first place, had rapidly turned into a hellish trek to… well, anywhere. The woman—Frances, had she said her name was?—owned the estate she'd stumbled onto, which had to include the barn, shed, whatever it was, that she'd crashed in… how long ago? Yet again, she had no idea. This was getting beyond a joke. Amnesia would have been less frustrating.

She went to speak, but a cough escaped instead. She clapped a hand over her mouth.

Without a word, Will retrieved a glass of water from the table beside her borrowed bed and handed it to her. Connie flashed him a weak smile of gratitude and started to gulp down the liquid, before remembering you were always supposed to sip in these situations, in case your stomach rebelled and you vomited. The last thing she wanted was to be sick in front of these nice people who'd helped her. Or worse—*on* them. She swallowed, then took a deep breath and then sipped carefully at the water until she'd had her fill.

"Here," Will said gently, "I'll take that."

"Thank you." Her smile was wider this time. "Sorry about that."

He shrugged and put the glass back where he'd got it from.

Feeling a tad less discombobulated now, Connie turned to Frances. "Thank you so much for your help and hospitality. I'm really sorry for trespassing on your land. I was…" God, how could she word this without letting her whole sorry story come tumbling out? "walking," *that* was the truth, at least, "when the weather turned horrid. I was nowhere near, well, anything, so when I saw the sign at the edge of your estate, I carried on, hoping I could take shelter in a shed or something." She remembered all but barging the door down. "I hope I haven't damaged anything. I'm happy to pay for any repairs." *As long as they only cost pennies, that is. My cash won't last very long otherwise.*

Frances gave a light chuckle and waved a dismissive hand. "It's fine, honestly. It was obvious when Will found you what had happened, clear you weren't up to anything nefarious. And there's no damage, so please dinnae worry about that. Are you up to a few questions?" She lifted her eyebrows expectantly.

"Um, yes." *As long as you don't ask me who I am or what I'm doing here. But of course, they're going to be your first bloody questions, aren't they? They'd certainly be mine, if our roles were reversed.* "I'll do my best," she added, figuring she could act all sleepy or dopey to buy her some time to answer if need be.

Smiling warmly, Frances continued, "First, and most important, how are you feeling? You'd been exposed to the elements for quite some time before Will came across you. We wanted to take you to hospital, or at the very least call a doctor, but you wouldnae let us. You were very insistent."

I wouldn't? She hoped she'd stifled her surprise. *Guess I'm determined to protect myself, even when I'm totally out of it.* "I, uh," heat bloomed in her cheeks, and she shifted uncomfortably beneath the bedclothes, "I'm feeling okay, I guess. Tired, and I ache all over, but it could have been worse, all things considered."

"Aye," Frances replied, sterner now. "It could have. You could have been suffering with hypothermia. You've been incredibly lucky. So, what's your name, honey? And why are you so petrified of doctors?"

Petrified of...? The penny dropped. Of course—that was the conclusion they'd drawn when she'd insisted she didn't want to go to hospital, or see a doctor. Still, it was better to let them keep believing that than have them know that, technically speaking, she was on the run and was desperate to keep her identity, her location, a secret.

And she *was* desperate. She didn't want *him* tracking her down, trying to persuade her to go back home with him. She wanted him out of her life for good, having put up with his shit for far too long. He'd find her eventually, she was sure, but she'd be stronger then, after some time away. More able to stand up for herself. To tell him to get lost and leave her alone. If she could just keep her identity under wraps, not leave or create any kind of trail leading to her, for as long as possible, everything would be all right. It *had* to be. She couldn't go back to how things were.

She forced herself to respond before she aroused their suspicions—if she hadn't done that already, that was. "My name's Connie Smith." The first name was accurate, of course, and she wasn't carrying any documents which proved the surname to be a lie. So they could either believe her, or not. Their choice. "And the doctor thing... well," she let out a humourless laugh to buy herself some time to come up with something, "let's just say I had a traumatic experience as a small child, and I've never quite got over it." They were total strangers, surely they wouldn't press her for any more information than that? She hoped not—the more complex lies became, the easier it was for them to trip you up. The key to getting out of the other side of this situation was keeping it simple.

Frances's pretty face creased into a sympathetic expression. "Oh, I'm sorry, honey. Connie," she corrected herself, "that must have been so awful for you. Of *course* you wouldn't want to see a doctor. Anyway, enough of that—you seem much better now. Out of the woods, as the saying goes."

"Yes." Connie nodded emphatically. "And I'll be out of your hair as soon as possible." She looked around, taking in more detail of the small room, and the fact the light filling it was artificial. The curtains were tightly closed, without a smidgen of brightness shining through or around them. It was night time, then. *Shit.* She couldn't very well take off in the dark—not unless she wanted to end up in this situation yet again, but perhaps without anyone finding her. Or someone dodgy finding her, or even someone unsympathetic to her plight and eager to turn her in to the police, who could well be looking for her, if *he'd* filed a missing person's report. Hopefully he hadn't. Hopefully his stupid masculine pride wouldn't have allowed it. It would mean people finding out she'd left him, after all. "Um, what time is it? What *day* is it, actually?" She scratched her head, immediately regretting it when she felt the state of the bird's nest which used to be her hair.

Will laughed, but not unkindly. "Bless ye, hen. Ye've had a bit of a time of it, haven't ye?" He pushed up the cuff of his well-worn sweatshirt and checked his watch. "It's almost half past eight. At night," he added, a twinkle in his blue eyes. "Ye cannae go anywhere now, lass. And it's Friday. I found ye on Wednesday. The Wednesday two days ago, that is."

Connie gaped at him. "Two *days* ago? I've been asleep for *two days?*" *No wonder I'm dying for a pee.*

"Aye." He nodded, which flipped some strands of his ginger hair into his eyes. He shoved them away with the impatient scrape of a hand. "Like Frances said, ye were in quite the state when I found ye. Wetter than a loch, shivering worse than anything I've ever seen, yer teeth chattering and all. I dumped all me tools where I stood and tried to help ye. Wake ye up—but ye were seriously out of it. I gave up in the end, just scooped ye up and brought ye back here. Thought it was for the best. Frances took over then—she got ye undressed and warmed ye up. And not a moment too soon, I reckon." He absentmindedly scratched his beard, the same burnished-copper colour as his hair, then gave a decisive nod. "I'm mighty glad ye are all right. Like Frances said, ye had us worried."

"Will's right," Frances put in, drawing Connie's attention back to her—a shame, really, as she much preferred looking at Will. "You can't go anywhere now. Well, you *can,* if you want. You're not a prisoner here, obviously. What I *mean* is, it's dark, it's cold, and it's wet. Surely wherever you need to be can wait until tomorrow? You're welcome to stay here another night. This room is spare at the moment anyway." She paused. "Is there anyone you need to call? Anyone who will be wondering where you are?"

Connie swallowed hard, hoping her voice wouldn't betray

her. She shook her head. "No. I don't need to call anyone." Well, that was true, at least. She deliberately ignored the second question, hoping Frances would think the answer Connie had just given covered that, too.

He would most definitely be wondering where she was, would be out looking for her. Her friends and family, on the other hand, wouldn't yet know anything was amiss. Not until the letter Connie had posted near King's Cross Station landed on the doormat at her mother's house, anyway. And that wouldn't have happened too quickly, given the sheer amount of post which went through the system in central London, plus she'd deliberately used a second-class stamp, buying herself some time to put plenty of distance between her and her home. Her old life.

She'd worked her week's notice at her job, so her boss—ex-boss, now—wouldn't be expecting to see her again. All ends were neatly tied up. Or at least as tied up as they could be when you'd done what Connie had done. Had a mental breakdown, then taken off and left everything behind.

She forced a smile. "Thank you. For everything. Again. And yes, if that's all right, I will stay another night. Then I'll be out of your way tomorrow morning."

Frances watched her for a moment or two, as though assessing her, then nodded slowly. "Of course. You're very welcome. And welcome to stay. There's no need to rush off tomorrow, though. Get up whenever you're ready. The clothes you were wearing have been laundered and dried, and everything in your bag has been dried." She gave a wry grin. "It wasn't just you and your clothes that got soaked through." Jerking her head towards a door off to her right, she went on, "Bathroom's through there. Plenty of hot water for a shower. In the morning, make sure you go down and get some breakfast. The kitchen is out of this door," she pointed behind her, "turn left and make your way to the end of the corridor, where you'll find the stairs. Go down to the ground floor, and the kitchen is your first door on the left. Whoever is in there will find you something to eat and drink. Then please, come and find me before you leave, just so I know you're all right. Okay?"

This time Connie couldn't stop her voice from trembling, just as she couldn't stop the tears pooling in her eyes, threatening to spill. "I, uh… thank you. I will. S-see you in the morning then, I guess."

Will cleared his throat, obviously uncomfortable, and jumped to his feet. "Right, well, I can see I'm no longer needed here, so I'll be on me way."

Connie watched as he tucked the chair he'd been sitting on up against the wall, then hurried to the door. Just before he disappeared, she called out, "Thank you, Will. For finding me… helping me."

He gave a curt nod. "Yer welcome, lass. I'd have done the same for anyone. Not good to be wandering these hills in filthy weather like that. Blowing a hoolie, it was. I'm just glad I found ye when I did. Sleep tight, and safe travels, wherever yer going."

He'd gone before she could respond. With raised eyebrows, she turned back to Frances, who'd also got up, but didn't appear to be in quite such a hurry to leave. "Eat your soup," she gestured to a tray Connie hadn't previously noticed on the dressing table, "then get some sleep. You know what they say—everything will look better in the morning. I can't guarantee the weather will conform—this is Scotland, after all—but you'll feel better after some more sleep and a nice, hot shower. Or a bath. Whatever you prefer. Like I said, there's plenty of hot water." She gave a one-shouldered shrug. "See you tomorrow, Connie. Sleep well."

"Y-yes, I will. Thank you." *God, how many times have I said thank you, now? I'm like a bloody parrot.*

But then, she realised, thank you was the very least she could say to the people who had, in all honesty, probably saved her life.

Chapter Two

Surprisingly, everything *did* look—and feel—better in the morning. Though that was most likely the result of spending the best part of two days tucked up in a warm, comfortable bed—despite not being aware of it for much of the time.

Connie's temporary bedroom was filled with light, and on this occasion, it had nothing to do with electricity or light bulbs. The sun forced its way through and around the fabric of the curtains, apparently trying to make everyone aware it had won the battle with the clouds and rain—for now, at least.

She let out a yawn and stretched, while psyching herself up to clamber from the warm, soft embrace of the bed. Just because things seemed better now didn't mean she relished the day ahead. She had no idea where she was going to go, or what she was going to do, for starters. That had been a perfectly acceptable state of affairs when she'd first taken off, since all she wanted to do was put as much distance as was physically possible between her and *him*. Now, though, she couldn't stop her brain from chiming in with questions:

Where will you go? Where will you sleep? Where will you wash yourself, your clothes? What will you eat? What will you do when your money runs out?

Unable to answer any of the questions, Connie growled at her own annoying—not to mention extremely concerning—thoughts, then reluctantly threw off the thick duvet and got up. Padding over to the en suite, she resolved to take things one step at a time to avoid becoming overwhelmed and sending herself into a panic. She wouldn't get *anything* done if she became paralysed by fear. Her mental state was fragile enough as it was.

First, use the bathroom. Then get cleaned up. Get dressed. Pack your bag. Leave this room in a tidy state. Go downstairs and find the kitchen to get some food. Then go and see Frances.

She stopped there, since there was nothing else beyond that. But that was seven things to do. Maybe if she did them all at a fairly languid pace, by the time she'd checked a few off, her brain would have supplied something to tack onto the end. Some kind of action plan. Or even just an action would do. Anything that wasn't nothing. Nothing was hopeless. Pointless. If she fell down that particular rabbit hole, she may as well turn around and head back to where she'd come from.

No. No way. I am a strong, intelligent, resourceful woman. I've got this far, which is an achievement in itself. He *is nowhere to be seen. I'm the one in control now. I can do this, make a new life for myself. People survive much worse situations than this—even thrive. And so will I. I'm not giving up.*

That decided, she worked her way through the first five items on her mental to-do list. Then she scooped up her rucksack, which she'd repacked with all her now-dry belongings, meagre as they were, and left the room.

Thanks to Gran and her sayings, Frances's instructions for finding the kitchen were easy to remember. She needed to turn left, head to the stairs, then the ground floor, and turn left again. So that's precisely what she did.

The smells and noises made it blindingly obvious she was in

the right place as she hovered outside the door. It was breakfast time, and judging by the cacophony coming from the kitchen, the hotel was busy with guests. Apparently the changeable weather of the Scottish Highlands didn't deter tourists. But then, she supposed, once you arrived somewhere on holiday, you were at the mercy of the weather. It just so happened that here the weather was often wet.

She took a deep breath and pushed open the door. Unsurprisingly, nobody noticed her. They certainly wouldn't have heard her enter over the din, and they were all so engrossed in their individual tasks that it'd take much more than someone slipping into the room to attract their attention. A marching band might just about do it.

She looked around, wondering who to approach. The trouble was, they all seemed frantically busy. They didn't need her interrupting their work in order to give them *more* work to do. She wasn't a paying guest, wasn't contributing to their wages. Why should they help *her*? But… Frances had been most insistent. *And she'd promised to find the woman once she'd eaten.* She'd need to speak to someone in order to find out where the owner's office was, so would it really be *that* much of an imposition to enquire about a slice of toast while she was at it? Maybe a hot drink?

As the steamy heat and irresistible food smells assaulted her, her stomach rumbled. *Guess that's that question answered, then.* The vegetable soup and bread rolls she'd eaten last night had been delicious, and had perked her up no end, but if she'd been asleep for two days then she'd missed several meals. Following her long, arduous journey—the last part of it on foot, as she'd been eager to avoid CCTV on buses, trains, and in town centres—her body probably needed more sustenance to make up for what she'd missed. Especially since she was heading back out into unfamiliar territory on what would likely be another arduous journey. Possibly several of them, until she ended up somewhere she might be able to settle. And who knew how long that would take?

Suck it up, Connie, and go and ask someone for some bloody toast. You can't stand here dithering all day.

She nodded, then looked around at the various members of staff, trying to figure out who appeared the least harassed. Quickly surmising they were all equally rushed off their feet, she attempted to pinpoint the kindest face. The person least likely to be pissed off by her interrupting them. *Christ, you never used to be this much of a wimp. All this time being under* his *thumb has done this to you. Turned you into some browbeaten little mouse. Well, no more. Time to turn things around, starting right now.*

Taking a deep breath, she moved out of the doorway and made her way further into the room. Several fleeting glances came her way, but since everyone was so focussed on getting breakfast to the hotel guests in a timely manner, nobody spoke, or approached her. She didn't take it personally.

Once she'd stepped forward a couple more paces, a part of the room previously hidden around a corner came into view. And there, much to her relief, was someone just standing there—a large man around her age, in chef's whites, his arms folded across his big barrel chest. He was keeping an incredibly watchful eye on what was going on around him, which told Connie there was a good chance he was the head chef—or at least the most senior member of kitchen staff currently on shift. He might also know all about her predicament, too, if he'd spoken to Frances. She hoped he had, so she wouldn't have to explain who she was and what she was doing there. He might not be too happy about her mooching around his domain, otherwise.

Mentally crossing her fingers, she picked her way across the room, trying her best not to get under the feet of the scurrying staff. She wanted to *eat* some food, not end up covered in it if she collided with someone.

By the time she reached the man in charge, he was alternating curious glances at her with continuing to keep a watchful eye on the kitchen's productivity.

"Hi," she said as she sidled up to him, then added a hopeful smile. "I-I'm Connie. I've been… er, *Frances* sent me. She told me I should come here and that someone would find me some breakfast. I-if it's not too much trouble." Her heart pounded as she awaited his response. Close up, he seemed even bigger, and although he hadn't so much as opened his mouth, she suspected he would be gruff and more than a little bit scary. God, what would it be like to have him as a boss? But then she reminded herself that *his* boss had sent her here, so hopefully everything would be okay. He was hardly going to grab a carving knife and chase her out of the kitchen.

Unfolding his arms didn't make him any less intimidating. But she found herself heaving a huge sigh of relief when his face softened and he held his hand out. Suddenly, he wasn't so bad. "I'm Craig Gemmell, and I know who ye are, lass. Dinnae worry—the boss filled me in. She says I'm to feed ye up until yer fit to pop, then send ye to her office." They shook—her hand almost disappearing entirely in his large, warm one.

"Oh," she gave a nervous smile, "I don't want to put anyone to any trouble. A slice or two of toast will do. Or even a bowl of cereal. I can help myself, if you let me know where it is."

"Och, nonsense! I willnae hear of it." He waved his hand to indicate the bustling space. "We're already feeding a small army—one more mouth is nae trouble at all, I promise ye that. Now, where would ye like to sit? We can squeeze ye in a corner of the dining room, with the guests, or ye can borrow me office, as long as ye dinnae make a mess on me desk."

"Your office would be great, thank you. I don't want to look like Billy-no-mates in the dining room. I promise I won't make a mess." Her smile was wider this time. She had a strong suspicion Craig Gemmell was, in fact, a gentle giant.

"Nae bother. So, what would ye like to eat? As ye can see, there's plenty on the go. A fried breakfast?" He rattled off a list of ingredients that was probably longer than his arm—and that was saying something.

She thought for a moment, trying to recall everything he'd just said. There had been a *lot* to take in. "Y…es to everything except the mushrooms, please."

He inclined his head. "Tea or coffee? Or juice? Or all of the above?" He grinned.

She mirrored his facial expression. "You're taking Frances's order literally, are you? About making me pop?"

"Aye. Why no'? Ye've had a hard couple of days—least I can do is make sure yer belly's full before ye leave us."

She dropped her gaze to the floor, suddenly overwhelmed by the kindness of these strangers she'd stumbled upon. They didn't know her, owed her nothing, and yet they'd looked after her, kept her safe, made her welcome. Apparently, she'd forgotten people could actually *be* nice. Even when they weren't getting anything in return.

Swallowing hard against the lump in her throat, she lifted her head and forced herself to meet Craig's gaze. "Thank you. From the bottom of my heart. I can't even find the words to let you know how grateful I am."

"Ahh, dinnae fash," he replied, a faint blush staining his cheeks. "I told ye, it's nae bother. I'm no' even cooking it for ye—I've got me minions here to do that for me." He winked. "Perks o' the job."

Connie chuckled. "Looks like a great place to work. From the little I've seen, anyway."

"Aye, it is. As a local lad, I might be a tad biased, but this hotel sits amongst the most beautiful countryside in the world. Tourists come from all over the globe, and I'm privileged to help fill *their* bellies, too. Speaking o' which, let's get ye settled in me office. And ye never said what ye wanted to drink. Come on, we'll get that now so ye can take it with ye."

"Tea would be great, please."

"Coming right up."

As Connie followed Craig over to a section off to one side of the kitchen where gleaming silver hot-water urns sat alongside teapots, cups and saucers, and various other drink-making accoutrements, a surprising sentiment hit her:

I really don't want to leave this place.

Chapter Three

Connie practically waddled along the corridor to Frances's office. Despite her protests, Craig had presented her with a large plate, piled high with delicious breakfast foods. And, much to his delight, Connie had demolished nearly all of it—hence the almost-waddling. She couldn't remember the last time she'd been so full up. Perhaps it was just because she'd been so empty to begin with, but an immense feeling of satisfaction settled over her even though she was, indeed, in danger of popping. Thank goodness her hiking trousers had an elasticated waistband.

With what felt like a superhuman effort, Connie lifted her hand and knocked on the door she'd arrived outside. A smart, brass sign fixed to it simply read *Frances McKenzie*.

"Come in," called a voice.

Connie opened the door and entered the room to find the woman in question ensconced behind an enormous, old-fashioned wooden desk, complete with dark-green leather inlay. A quick glance around confirmed the beautiful desk fit in perfectly with its equally old-fashioned surroundings. She wondered if the entire hotel was like this—classic, elegant, stunning. After all, she'd only seen the staff quarters—which were modern, clean and serviceable—and the kitchens—which were all gleaming stainless-steel and white tile. Would the public areas, the guest rooms, all be like this? She'd planned to head off as soon as she'd spoken to Frances, but now she found herself hoping for a tour of the building. She hadn't yet decided what she was going to do next, where she was going to go, so hanging around Bowdley Hall Hotel a little longer wouldn't make the slightest bit of difference, would it?

"Ah, Connie," Frances said warmly, her wide smile matching her tone. "I was hoping it would be you. Come and sit down."

"Hi. Good morning," she replied, returning the smile. She closed the door, then shuffled over to the seat Frances had indicated, dropped her backpack down next to it, then lowered herself gingerly. She half-expected the chair to break under the weight of her and her enormous fried breakfast.

"Good morning. How are you feeling? Rested? Full up, I hope?" She lifted an eyebrow in query.

Nodding, she replied, "I'm feeling well, thank you. Extremely rested. As for the full up part… I think I went way past that. Craig gave me enough breakfast to feed a family of four." She rubbed her belly. "I feel like I'm the size of a baby whale or something."

Frances's laugh rang out, throaty and joyous, and Connie couldn't help smiling in response. It was infectious. "That sounds like Craig, all right. It's taken me years to get his portion size under control—it was costing us a small fortune to begin with. But it seems he made an exception for you." She shrugged. "But then, I did explain you were a special guest and that he was to look after you. Feed you up."

"Well, he certainly did that. I've got enough in my belly to keep me going for a week, I should think. Thank you so much for that, I really appreciate it. And again, thank you for your hospitality. Can I…?" She wondered how to word what she wanted to say. She couldn't possibly offer to pay the going rate for the bed and board—

whatever that might be—because that would wipe out a considerable chunk of her cash in one fell swoop, cash she currently had no means of replenishing. But at the same time, she didn't feel she could just walk away without having contributed *somehow*. It would be taking advantage.

Finally, her brain supplied a solution. "Can I repay you somehow? I, er, don't have a lot of money…" she carried on, ignoring the heat in her cheeks, "but I'd be more than happy to do something else for you. Maybe help your housekeeping staff out for a few hours—or however long you see fit? I can change beds, empty bins, whatever."

Shaking her head, Frances said, "No, no, that's not necessary, Connie. Please, don't give it another thought. The room you slept in wasn't being used anyway, and a wee bit of electricity and hot water, and a couple of meals aren't exactly going to bankrupt me. You clearly needed help, and I was more than happy to give it."

"And *I'm* more than happy to work until I've paid off my debt to you," Connie replied, the words tumbling from her lips before her brain even had time to think them through. What the hell was *wrong* with her? The woman was being nice, letting her off the hook, and here she was trying to get herself back *on* the damn hook. What kind of person was eager to work when they didn't have to?

The kind of person who has nowhere else to go, that's who.

Frances had been about to say something else when she caught sight of Connie's expression. She closed her mouth, then narrowed her eyes as she continued to study Connie, who was shrinking further into the chair with every passing second. *Why didn't you just keep quiet? Say thank you and be on your way, like you promised? Now she thinks you're a loony. She'll be calling Security to have you thrown out any minute. So much for paying her back.*

Letting out a long breath, Frances ceased her intense scrutiny of Connie and turned her attention to the window. As she stared out at the rolling Scottish Highlands, her face softened, then turned thoughtful again. With a gentle smile, she returned her attention to Connie. "All right, if you mean what you say about wanting to repay me, then I have a suggestion. Answer me this question honestly: are you in some kind of trouble?"

"Err…" She really *didn't* want to lie to this woman. As well as having been incredibly kind to her, she was clearly shrewd and wouldn't believe any bullshit Connie might be able to come up with on the fly. But how *could* she answer the question honestly without making things a hundred times worse?

As Frances waited, her lifted eyebrows making her expectation of a response painfully clear, Connie fidgeted in her seat, frantically scrambling for a suitable reply.

It seemed the silence and awkward eye contact were too much for Frances, because she sat forward in her seat, placed her hands on the desktop, and said firmly, "Connie, your body language and demeanour are answering the question for you, loud and clear. Not to mention the circumstances of you being here in the first place. So why not just tell me? I realise I'm a total stranger, but I am *also* a total stranger who has kept you safe and respected your wishes when you didn't want me to take you to a hospital or call a doctor when really, for the sake of your health, I should have. I'm not going to judge you. As long as you haven't committed some heinous crime, nobody else even needs to know what you tell me. But if you *don't* tell me, I can't help you."

"I never *asked* you to help me," she shot back. God, the last thing she needed was to be even further in debt to this woman.

"Christ on a bike, you're a right pain in the arse!" She cast her eyes heavenward and threw up her hands before meeting Connie's gaze again. "I'm beginning to wish Will had left you out in the bloody rain. I *know* you never asked. You've never asked for a damn thing, since you've been here. But I've got eyes in my head, as well as a brain between my ears, lass. I *know* something is wrong. You're running from something, or someone, and I'm in a position to help you. I don't just mean giving you a bed for a few nights and a couple of meals, either. This place is mine, remember?" She lifted a hand, palm up, indicating their surroundings. "I can do whatever the hell I like, and anyone who questions me can piss right off. Not that anyone would dare." She smirked. "Except for you, apparently. But then, I'm not paying your wages… yet."

Connie frowned. What on earth was this nutty Scotswoman going on about now? Paying her wages? After a couple of seconds, the penny dropped. "Y-you're offering me a job?" she almost squeaked. *How does she even know I need a job? Is she bloody psychic, or something?*

"If you want it. On one condition," Frances replied coolly.

"Which is...?"

"Tell me what's going on. And no bullshit. You owe me this

much." She smiled thinly.

Connie sighed and slumped back in her chair, immediately regretting it when the hard wood dug into her back. This piece of furniture, beautiful as it was, had been made for functionality, not for comfort. "You're right, I do. I'm not in trouble, exactly, but I *am* running from someone. And I really, *really* don't want him to find me. Not *ever*." She didn't stamp her foot, not quite, but the emphasis was clear and filled the room with its presence.

"All right… Tell me more. Oh, wait—hold that thought. Shall we have a wee drink to go with our chat? I could do with more caffeine. You?"

"Yes, that would be lovely, thanks."

"Tea, coffee, something else?"

"Tea, if it's not too much trouble."

"None at all." She pressed a button on the phone on her desk—a piece of kit which looked impossibly modern against the antique desk—waited until someone responded, then said, "Elsa, could I get a pot of tea in here, please? Two cups. Thank you."

"Aye, coming right up," said the disembodied voice, then there was a soft *click*.

"Right. While we're waiting, you might as well start. She'll knock before she comes in, so she won't overhear anything you say. Our conversation from here on out will be completely confidential. And just so you know, Craig only knows the bare minimum about how you came to be here, and he won't gossip. Will won't breathe a word, either."

"Okay. I…" She sighed again. "Sorry, give me a second. I'm

not quite sure *where* to start, to tell you the truth."

"The beginning usually works."

Connie couldn't help but smile. Frances was incredibly quick, and witty. She'd have to watch herself, especially since the woman was, apparently, about to become her boss. Getting on the wrong side of her would be incredibly unwise. "Very true. But we might be here for a while."

Frances tilted her head. "Not a problem—I've got all day."

After thinking for a moment, Connie said, "Well, I suppose it's like a fairy tale, but in reverse. So rather than having a happily ever after, it was a happily ever beginning." She shook her head. "That sounds stupid now I've said it out loud, but you know what I mean. Anyway, it started out wonderfully, and ended up turning into a big, steaming pile of shit." She cringed. "Excuse my language."

With a chuckle, Frances said, "No excuses needed. As long as you don't swear in front of guests, go for your life. I swear like a trooper, myself. So, what is this mysterious *it* you're referring to? A relationship?"

"Yes. I won't go into every single detail—it'll bore you to death. I'll just give the pertinent points. So, we met, we dated, we fell in love, we moved in together. All was well. Great, in fact. Life was wonderful. He paid me attention, complimented me, was affectionate. We spent time together—both quality time at home, and fun days and nights out. We got on well, made each other laugh." She paused for breath. Wow, it seemed now she'd started, it was all pouring out of her. "We never argued. I mean *never*. Not so much as a cross word. Some might say that came from a lack of passion, but I disagree. We just seemed to have no *reason* to argue."

Frances inclined her head. "It happens."

"Sure does. Anyway, as with most things in life, everything was brilliant… until it wasn't. I'd just started a new job—at a new place, in a higher position than my previous job. Better pay, more prospects. Another positive point in my already wonderful life. Unfortunately, though, it changed everything. I'm still not sure how, or why. After a while, he became snappy whenever I talked about work, or my colleagues. I'd begun to fit in, make friends. They were a sociable lot, and I started going out with them for the occasional drink after work, or for a quick pub lunch. It seemed to make him irritable. I suppose he was jealous, because I was spending time with them, rather than him. Though meeting him for lunch was totally impractical because our workplaces were much too far apart. Maybe he was even jealous of my success, because my job was a step up from the previous one.

"Anyway, it went on for a while, with him being grumpy whenever I mentioned my colleagues. So I stopped—it just seemed easier. But when I did that, he started *asking* about them. Had I been out with them? Where had we been? What did we do? And then he'd be unresponsive and disinterested when I replied. It was mind-boggling. We never used to argue, and now here he was, *trying* to pick fights with me. Like he desperately *wanted* to argue." She stopped speaking when a knock came at the door. Their tea had arrived.

When Elsa had closed the door behind her again, Connie continued as Frances poured the drinks. "I'm telling this story with hindsight, which of course is 20/20. I tolerated it for a while, because I loved him. But I see now his behaviour changed me. I became quieter, stopped socialising as much—though I was hardly a party animal to begin with—you get the idea. Whether it was intentional or not, I guess I'll never know, but he wore me, wore my personality down, until I just became this quiet little mouse, this sad person. It wasn't even as if I was having fun with *him* anymore—so it's not like he got to spend more quality time with me as a result of all this. I just got up, went to work, did my job, came home, ate, showered, watched TV, went to bed, slept. Rinse and repeat. Day after day. Like a bloody zombie. We barely spoke to each other, and I grew increasingly depressed because I didn't know what was wrong, so I couldn't figure out how to fix it. Eventually, I plucked up the courage to broach the subject. Let's just say he *wasn't* impressed. He refused to discuss it, refused to take in what I was saying, let alone respond to it. I gave up in the end. It just made him even more irritable, and it got to the stage where I was scared of him. Scared of that glint in his eye whenever I said something he didn't like. He'd never so much as raised his voice at me before all this happened, but now things were different. *He* was different, and he'd made me into a different person, too. He screamed, he shouted, he threw things and punched walls. Things had become so volatile, that I was just… afraid. Afraid of the day when he'd lash out at *me* instead of inanimate objects. And even if he never did, I knew I simply couldn't live like that anymore. My mental health had declined massively, and I'd had enough. So I plucked up the courage to leave. I worked my notice at my job, posted a letter to my mother—my dad's not in the picture—when I was passing through London so she wouldn't worry too much and… well… here I am."

Chapter Four

There was a long silence where Frances seemed to be mulling over Connie's words. Understandable, really, since there had been a *lot* of them. Connie kept quiet, but her heart pounded as she waited with increasing anxiety for the other woman's response. She killed time by adding milk and sugar to her tea and stirring it.

Eventually, after taking a sip of tea and replacing the cup back onto its saucer, Frances met Connie's eyes and gave a nod. "Not that it's for me to comment, but I think you did the right thing. Leaving him, I mean. Maybe the running away part was a bit extreme, leaving your belongings, home, and job behind, but you obviously felt you had no other option. Better that than ending up in a psychiatric unit. At least your mother is aware, so there hopefully won't be any missing person's reports going out. I suspect you don't want your face splashed all over the media. Anyway, what's done is done. Moving forward is the only way now. So what I propose is this: work here, live here, hide out here. Nobody else has to know your real name, or that there's anything amiss. That'll be between me and you. As long as you do your job to the best of your ability, I'm perfectly happy for you to stay here until you get back on your feet. And then what you do next is your choice. But I'll support you however I can. How does that sound?"

"How does that…?" Connie shook her head, incredulous. "It *sounds* like a dream come true, that's what! Once again, I can't thank you enough." She blew out a heavy breath. "God, I really got lucky when I trespassed on your land, didn't I?"

"That you did," Frances replied, the ghost of a smile flitting across her lips. "If you'd been but a mile or so to the east, things would have been very different. The landowners would have been more likely to shoot you than take you in. And I hear they're fond of taxidermy."

Connie gasped, then giggled when she caught sight of the twinkle in Frances's eye. "So… what happens now?"

"Well, I guess we should get you settled in, if you're going to be around a while. The room you stayed in the past few days is now yours for the duration. I do need an extra pair of hands in the housekeeping department, so the job I'm offering you is as a chambermaid. I'll get you a uniform sorted as soon as possible. Assuming that's all right with you?"

Nodding frantically, Connie said, "Yes, yes, of course. You're saving my life here—I'll do anything." She picked up her tea and drank.

"Good. Right, how would you like a tour? I'll show you around and introduce you to as many other members of staff as I can along the way. You'll find them a friendly, welcoming bunch. I'm guessing you don't really know the area, but we really are very remote here, so the vast majority of the staff live on site. That means we're a close-knit group. Sometimes disagreements happen, of course, but for the most part we work hard and play hard." She shrugged. "As long as all the work gets done, and done well, and my guests are happy, then I'm happy. I'm no slave driver. I offer good, honest pay for good, honest work. I encourage everyone to come to me with any issues, and I'll always do what I can to rectify them. Morale is important, especially in a place like this where we often have to make our own entertainment. Don't get me wrong, we've got all the mod cons—WiFi, TVs, a staff games room, as well as access to the gym, pool, and sauna—but it's easy to get a little cabin fever being stuck within the same four walls day in, day out."

Frances chuckled. "That makes it sound terrible—you'll be running away again if I keep on like that, won't you? I'm giving the impression that sleeping in an outbuilding is preferable. Trust me, it's not. Right, I'll stop telling you, and just *show* you, instead. Then you can make up your own mind. All right?"

Connie had been alternating nods and sips of her tea as Frances spoke, and now she nodded again. "Yes, that sounds like a good idea to me." She finished her drink and replaced the cup. "I'm ready when you are."

"Excellent." She rose from her chair, then walked over to the door and opened it. "After you."

"Thank you." Connie got up and passed through the door, then waited as Frances locked up behind them.

Catching her look of confusion as she turned, Frances said, "It's just a precaution—nothing to worry about." She pocketed the key. "I trust everyone who works for me implicitly, but it's not impossible for guests to find themselves in this corridor, and I don't want *them* snooping around my office now, do I? Plus, your bag's in there, isn't it?"

Connie wondered what exactly they might *find* if they snooped—it had looked perfectly innocuous to her—but said nothing. And she didn't particularly want anyone poking around in her belongings, meagre as they were. "Of course not."

"Come on then, let's show you everything Bowdley Hall Hotel has to offer." With that, she strode off down the thickly-carpeted corridor, her heels sinking into the pile with every step. Apparently nothing else in this corridor was worth seeing, since they didn't stop at any of the doors lining it. Instead, they continued to the end, then turned into another passageway running at right angles from the original one.

Connie blinked—she was already getting turned around, and couldn't remember where the kitchen was, or the stairwell which would lead her back to the bedroom that was apparently now hers for as long as she wanted it. She needed a map. Hopefully she'd get used to it soon enough, though.

Frances halted outside a door, then turned and winked at Connie. "I'm going to show you the fun stuff first." With that, she opened the heavy wooden door to reveal a large, light room, which Connie quickly realised was because of the glass rooflights breaking up the ceiling. Light spilled down onto a pool table, on which two men played—though they'd stopped and were currently looking hers and Frances's way. They wore jeans and T-shirts, so clearly weren't on duty. "Connie, this is the staff games room. And these two gentlemen are Nico Moretti," she indicated the man on the left, then the one on the right, "and Ashley Fox. Nico is one of our porters, and Ashley works as a waiter in the restaurant. Guys, this is Connie Smith—she's going to be working with us, filling the vacancy in our housekeeping department. I'm giving her the grand tour."

Temporarily pushing aside her sudden realisation that Frances had clocked on that Smith was not her real surname but had used it anyway—*wow, talk about slow on the uptake, Connie*—she smiled and waved shyly at both men, who looked to be a handful of years younger than her. "Hi. It's nice to meet you."

Ashley spoke first. "You too, Connie." He was attractive; tall and slim, with a mess of dark-blond hair, and brown eyes.

"Good to have you on board," Nico added, idly bouncing the end of his pool cue on the floor. Even if his name hadn't given it away, it was clear he had some Mediterranean heritage. He was traditionally handsome, as well as shorter and thicker set than his colleague, with hair so dark it was almost black, and brown eyes.

"Right," Frances said brightly, clasping her hands together. "We'll leave you gentlemen to continue your game." She turned her attention back to Connie. "So, as you can see, we have a pool table in here. Over there," she indicated two large tables set either side of a beautiful marble fireplace, "we have spaces available to play board games. There are chess and chequers boards, as well as the other usual suspects—Scrabble, Monopoly, and so on." She paused to take a breath, then pointed to a door set in the wooden panelling at the end of the room opposite an enormous picture window. "In there we have the cinema room. No windows or rooflights, for obvious reasons. There's a huge collection of DVDs and Blu-rays, as well as access to the streaming services. We won't go in, just in case someone's watching something."

A little overwhelmed, Connie nodded. If these were the luxuries the *staff* was afforded, what on earth was available to the paying guests? She forced a smile. "Sounds wonderful." Then, suddenly eager to get away from the inquisitive glances of Ashley and Nico, she added, "So, where next?"

Frances wrinkled her nose. "The laundry room, I'm afraid. Not nearly so much fun as this one. However, it's nearby and the staff are wonderful. Come on." With a nod to the two men, she ushered Connie out of the room.

The laundry turned out to be a couple of doors down, but on the opposite side of the corridor. Frances pushed open the door and both women were swallowed into a hive of activity, all bustle, noise, and the familiar, soothing scent of clean linen. "Right," Frances said, "let's go and organise you something to wear." She eyed Connie for a moment. "You're of average height, so length won't be an issue, but you've an ample bosom, if you don't mind me saying, so that might be more of a problem. Still, I'm sure we can sort something out for the short term, while your new uniform is on order."

There wasn't much she could say to that, so she trailed silently behind Frances as she made a beeline for a woman over to one side of the cavernous space. She was older than most of the others—who looked as though they ranged from their early twenties to around Connie's age—middle-aged, and clutched an iPad in one hand, the other stabbing irritably at the screen. As they drew closer, Connie caught the occasional utterance, "Confounded bloody machine... Nothing wrong with a clipboard... *Come on, I pressed that already!*"

She compressed her lips to prevent a smirk as she and Frances approached. Once the woman noticed them, her annoyed expression melted away and she became sweetness and light. The iPad was abandoned on the nearest flat surface. "Good morning,

Frances. What can I do for you?"

Indicating Connie, she replied, "Morning, Aileen. I have a new starter here. Chambermaid. Can you rustle her up a uniform for tomorrow while I get her measured for a new one and order it?"

Connie felt like a prime piece of meat as her figure was eyed up for the second time in as many minutes.

The woman—Aileen, Connie remembered, then committed the name to memory—narrowed her eyes thoughtfully, then nodded. "Aye, I think we've something that will fit the lass. Won't be ideal, though, so you'll want to get the new uniform on a rush job."

"Of course," Frances replied. "Anyway, I'm forgetting my manners. I apologise, ladies. Aileen, this is Connie. Connie, this is Aileen Taylor—she heads up this department, so your paths will cross a great deal."

"Hi, Aileen," Connie said, smiling. "It's lovely to meet you. And thank you for sorting out something for me to wear. I appreciate it."

"Good to meet you too, lass. And it's nae bother. Will you come to collect it, or shall I bring it up to you?"

Connie turned wide eyes on Frances, who put in, "Connie will be tied up with me for the rest of the day as I give her the tour and get her orientated. Would you mind dropping it off outside my office?"

"O' course," Aileen said. "I'll get on to that right away."

Once they'd finished their tour of the laundry and once again emerged into the corridor, Connie couldn't help wondering at the accents she'd heard. Surprisingly, since they were, apparently, in a very remote area of the Highlands, not everyone even *had* a Scottish accent. And those that did, sounded different from one another. Will, for example, had such a broad accent she practically needed subtitles to understand him. Frances had an unmistakeable Scottish accent, but it was soft, and she used only occasional slang. Craig was almost as undecipherable as Will, but had seemed to tone it down for her benefit. Ashley and Nico hadn't said very much, but unless she just hadn't picked it up, the two of them weren't Scottish at all. And then there was Aileen, whose accent was somewhere in between Will's and Frances's.

She guessed it was all down to their backgrounds and where they'd been born and brought up. Not all English people sounded the same, after all—far from it. Will had probably been born and brought up in Scotland, and rarely left the area, so there'd been nothing to rub any edges off his thick accent. Frances clearly not only *had* money, but *came* from money—so maybe she'd been educated outside of Scotland. London, perhaps? Maybe even further afield. And she'd likely travelled a lot, too.

As for the others, well, hopefully she'd find out in the fullness of time. If she stuck around long enough. Currently, she could see no reason *not* to—like Frances had said, everyone seemed friendly and welcoming, and she was filling a vacancy, so providing she did her job well, it would be hers for as long as she wanted it.

Just then, they turned a corner into yet another corridor. Only this one, rather than continuing with the wood-panelling décor she'd seen throughout, broke with tradition and had the roof and one side made entirely from glass. This, naturally, provided an excellent view of the landscape they were nestled within, and currently the weather was playing ball. The sun bathed the majestic hills—or were they mountains?—around them with light, as well as highlighting the grass, trees and plants in the valley bottom in which the hotel sat. Connie couldn't remember seeing so many shades of green before. It was dramatic, utterly spectacular, and although, deep down, she knew it probably wouldn't be this wonderful when it was blowing a hoolie, as Will had said—and of course, she had first-hand experience of *that*—she currently couldn't think of a single place she'd rather be.

"It's breathtaking, isn't it?" came Frances's voice from next to her.

Connie turned to face her new boss, nodding emphatically. "It really is. I can see why the Highlands are such a popular tourist destination. This is just stunning. No wonder you chose to live and work here."

"Oh, I didn't choose it," Frances replied simply, shaking her head, an expression of serenity and satisfaction on her face. "It chose *me*."

Chapter Five

The following morning, after a couple of false starts and a whole load of grumbling to herself, Connie eventually found the staff dining room. She was due to report to her line manager in the housekeeping department at 9 a.m., so she'd deliberately headed down for breakfast earlier than she needed to, so she didn't have to rush—and it gave her a buffer in case she got lost.

A handful of heads swivelled in her direction as she entered the room, and she swallowed down her nerves, forcing a polite smile at nobody in particular. Okay, now she'd found the dining room, she needed the kitchen. She knew where the kitchen was from her room, of course, but now she had to work out where it was in relation to *here*. And then make her way back again once she'd got something to eat, preferably without her food going cold. Maybe cereal would be a better idea today. A vision of herself eating a bowl of cornflakes in a corridor floated into her head.

Shit, I should have given myself an extra half an hour.

She turned and headed back out of the door, where she almost collided with a tall, dark-clad figure. A familiar figure. "Will!"

He frowned at her for a moment, then his face brightened. "Connie! I didnae recognise ye at first, lass. Sorry, I'm still half asleep here. Frances mentioned ye were sticking around. Chambermaid, eh?" He flicked his gaze along the length of her body, lingering for a millisecond too long on the chest area. She could hardly blame him, though—he was a red-blooded male, and the fitted black dress with its white collar and cuffs *was* rather snug around her boobs. Still, Frances had put a rush on a new one in her size, so hopefully it'd arrive soon and she'd be able to breathe a little easier—literally.

Resisting the temptation to cross her arms over the offending area and draw even more attention to it, she smiled. "Yes. Frances mentioned there was a vacancy, so here I am!" She'd given him the barest of the bare bones of her story, and mentally crossed her fingers he wouldn't ask any questions. Given he'd found her on the estate in the first place, he could be forgiven for any curiosity he had about her going from trespassing on Frances's property to working for her in the space of a couple of days.

Fortunately, he either wasn't curious, or was perceptive enough to realise she didn't want to talk about it. With a nod, he said, "Well, in that case, welcome. It's a good place to work, is this. Frances is a tough but fair boss. As long as ye get yer work done, and are polite and helpful to the guests, she'll be pleased wi' ye. Most everyone else is friendly, too. Ye've only to ask, and folks will be glad to help ye."

"It's good you said that, Will. Because I'm wondering if you could help me find the kitchens. I've come down for breakfast before my first shift, and obviously I've found the staff dining room, but now I need to find my way to the kitchens from here. This place is huge—I keep getting lost. I need a satnav."

Will chuckled, and indicated the corridor in front of him. "Dinnae fash, lass. I'd be happy to assist ye. I cannae promise I'll be any kind of satnav—I certainly dinnae have the posh voice—but I'll get ye to the kitchen and back, nae bother, since I'm going that way meself. Come wi' me."

Fifteen minutes later, they were settled back in the staff dining room with plates of food and hot drinks. The food portion wasn't nearly as big as the one she'd had the day before—but she'd gone from guest to employee, so it was fair enough. She *was* still getting free meals, after all. Besides, she didn't want to waddle away after eating like she had yesterday—the amount she had in front of her right now was more than enough to satisfy, to set her up for what would no doubt be a busy day.

Will picked up his knife and fork and jerked his head towards her plate. "Another perk o' the job is the meals. Ye dinnae have to cook it yeself, ye get more than enough, and it doesnae cost ye a penny." He cut a rasher of bacon in half, severed off a bite-sized piece of sausage, then speared them both on his fork. "Delicious, too." He flashed her a grin, then began eating.

Connie followed suit, and since they were both too busy eating to chat, took the opportunity to surreptitiously check out the other diners. Other than Will, she hadn't seen anyone she knew by name this morning. She recognised a few faces from her whistle-stop tour of the hotel the previous day, and either remembered or could tell from their uniforms whereabouts in the building they worked, but hadn't been introduced to any of them. But then, given the size of the place and the number of guest rooms, there had to be a huge number of employees to keep up with it all around the clock. Hopefully after a few days she'd have met and talked to more of her new colleagues, and their names would start to sink in. Name badges would help in that department, thankfully, since anyone who ever came into contact with guests was required to wear one. Apparently hers was on order along with her new uniform. For now, she was anonymous.

Will's voice broke into her thoughts. "Ye all right, lass? Ye look as though ye've the weight o' the world on yer shoulders."

"Sorry, yes, I'm fine. Just thinking about how I'm going to remember people's names, and find my way around this place."

He waved his fork a little, then used it to scoop up some baked beans. "Ye'll soon get used to it. And, like I said, if ye *do* get lost, just ask someone and they'll point ye in the right direction. I can give ye a guided tour o' the gardens too, if ye like. Not that it will help wi' yer work, o' course, but it's beautiful out there, even if I do say so meself. I'd like the opportunity to show it off to ye." He popped the forkful of beans into his mouth, his blue eyes glinting.

Connie hurriedly dropped her gaze to her plate, then poked the tines of her fork into a piece of fried bread, then a chunk of sausage. Was Will… *flirting* with her? She put the food in her mouth and began chewing, hardly tasting it as her mind wandered. It wasn't as though he'd said anything inappropriate—in fact he appeared to just be being nice—but it was the *way* he'd said it, the way his eyes had lingered a little too long on hers, the way he'd smiled at her. She could be barking up entirely the wrong tree, of course. It had been so long since anyone had shown any interest in her, much less flirted with her, that she'd forgotten what it was like.

She pushed the notion away. It didn't matter if he *was* flirting, if he *was* interested, because there was no way she was going there. Will was attractive—very much so, if she allowed herself to think about it. Not to mention kind, and helpful. But she'd run the length of the country—technically into another country, for God's sake—to get away from one man, leaving everything and everyone she knew and cared about behind. She wasn't about to get entangled with another bloke now, particularly as she'd been so lucky and landed on her feet here. She didn't want to ruin things. It might have only been a couple of days—if she just counted the ones where she'd been awake—but she really liked it here, and wanted to stay.

So, she'd keep her head down, work hard, save the wages she earned—which, to be fair, wouldn't be difficult since she wasn't paying for board or food—and live a quiet life here for as long as she wanted to. She'd be friendly to everyone, but remain cautious, guarded. Keep people at arm's length. Close friendships would inevitably lead to sharing information, building confidences, and how could she expect anyone to do that with her if she wouldn't divulge anything about herself? She certainly didn't want to go around telling lies—that simply wasn't her style. Nor was it very nice for anyone concerned.

She'd been so lost in her internal ramblings that she hadn't taken in what was going on around her. So she was surprised when Will's voice broke into her thoughts: "Right, that's me done, lass." He placed his knife and fork down on his plate with a clink. "I've got to get going now. I hope yer first day goes well, and remember what I told ye about asking for help. Dinnae be afraid."

She blinked stupidly for a moment as her brain scurried to catch up and process his words. "Er… yes," she finally managed, then forced a smile. "Thank you for being my satnav—albeit without the posh accent." She *didn't* add that she actually loved his accent, his gruff voice, and could happily listen to him talk all day. Read out the phone book, even. That wouldn't exactly count as keeping him at arm's length, would it? "And yes, I'll remember. Have a good day."

Will gave a curt nod, then stood and collected his plate and coffee mug. "Aye. Be sure that ye do." Then he turned and left the room, his long legs eating up the distance like it was nothing. She imagined he cut quite the imposing figure when he strode around the gardens and the estate.

Connie stared after him, still not entirely sure what had just happened. *Had* he been coming on to her, or had she got the wrong end of the stick? He hadn't said anything else, even when she hadn't responded to him. But to be fair, he hadn't actually asked her a question, he'd just made a suggestion. *Suggested* she might like a guided tour of the gardens. Not *asked* her. So maybe he hadn't been waiting for a response. Or perhaps he had, and was just too polite to press the issue. Or embarrassed. Or…

She let out a heavy sigh. She didn't have the time or the energy for this. A glance at her watch told her she needed to report to her new boss in twenty-five minutes. At the rate she was going, she'd spend at least half of that trying to *find* her damn boss. *Shit.*

Pushing everything else out of her head, she concentrated on finishing her meal, purposely ignoring the occasional glances that were thrown her way.

Luck was on her side, and she managed to return her used crockery to the kitchen, find her way back to her room, brush her teeth and *then* locate the housekeeping department, with five minutes to spare. Granted, she was breathing a little heavily as she entered the room and looked wildly around for her new line manager, but she was there, on time, and that was all that mattered for now. Baby steps.

"Are you all right?" The voice came from her right-hand side.

Startled, Connie gasped and turned to see a pale face peering from behind a tall shelving unit. The blonde woman, who appeared to be a couple of years younger than her, smiled. "Oh, hi," she replied, attempting to return the smile, with no idea if she'd succeeded or was simply grimacing, "I-I'm the new chambermaid, and I'm looking for Isla. I—"

The woman stepped out, a pack of toilet rolls in one hand, and a box of what looked to be mini bottles of shampoo in the other. "Connie, is it?" Her smile widened. "I'm Lisa—we'll be working together. Come on, I'll help you find Isla. She's in here somewhere, and I know she's expecting you." She put her burdens down on a nearby housekeeping cart, and headed further into the space, which was filled with shelving units holding everything one would expect to see in a housekeeping department—and some things one wouldn't.

Before Connie could give any thought to what *exactly* a bumper box of large-sized flavoured condoms was doing sitting innocuously on a shelf, Lisa spoke. "Ah, here we are. Isla, your new starter is here."

A tall woman in her fifties glanced up from the laptop she

was tapping away at with a smile. "Ah, Connie. Glad you found us okay. I know this place can be intimidating and confusing when you first arrive. Almost everyone gets lost. Thanks, Lisa." She gave the other woman a nod, then rose from her chair and held out her hand. Connie shook it, hoping her palm wasn't too sweaty. "I'm Isla. Pleased to have you on board. Your arrival's a wee bit… unexpected, not to mention I usually sit in on interviews with people who are applying for jobs in this department, but Frances tells me your circumstances are unusual. And we *do* need the help. We've a full house, so to speak, so lots of rooms to clean and look after."

Connie's heart pounded. What had Frances told her? She'd assured Connie she'd keep the details of her arrival at the hotel strictly confidential.

Isla waved a dismissive hand. "Oh, dinnae worry yourself—I'm not about to start questioning you or your credentials. Frances has vouched for you, and that's plenty good enough for me. She has very high standards, so I'm confident you'll live up to her expectations. Not right away, o' course, but once you've settled in, you'll be just fine, I'm sure. This job is hard work, but it isnae rocket science, so you'll pick it up in no time. For the time being, I've got ye working with Lisa," she jerked her head in the direction the other woman had gone, "and she'll see ye right. Any questions, you ask her, or me. We dinnae bite." She chuckled and patted Connie on the arm. "Go on then, lass, off wi' ye. There's chambermaiding to be done."

After swallowing hard in an attempt to combat her dry mouth, Connie said, "T-thank you. I'm a hard worker, and I'm good at taking direction. I won't let you, or Frances, down."

"Glad to hear it, hen. Have a good day."

Connie inclined her head, then spun on her heel and went in search of Lisa. She had a feeling the other woman had been hanging around the department deliberately waiting for her, so she didn't want to hold her up, put her behind with her work. She was here to help, not hinder.

She soon found Lisa not two paces away from where she'd first seen her. The cart she'd been loading now looked full to bursting. "All done?" she asked when Connie approached. Connie nodded. "Good. Am I right in thinking you haven't done this sort of work before?"

"No. I mean yes, that's right."

"Okay. I just wanted to make sure I'm not teaching you to suck eggs."

Shaking her head, Connie replied, "Not at all. Don't worry. Like I just told Isla, I'm a hard worker and I take direction well."

"Excellent. So," Lisa indicated the cart, "we normally have one of these each, but since you'll be with me for a few days, we'll be sharing. As I'm sure you've worked out, we have everything we need in or on here to either clean a room for remaining guests, or turn a room over completely for new guests. Bedding, towels, toilet rolls, tissues, cleaning supplies and so on. So basically we load this bad boy up at the beginning of a shift, and away we go. Little tip for you: if you collect or get given a cart and it looks as though someone's already filled it, for God's sake *check*. Trust me on that one—you'll save yourself a ton of time and potential headaches.

Trust only your own eyes and brain. Or mine, in this case. All right?"

Connie nodded again. "Noted."

"Great." She grabbed an iPad from the top of the cart and moved to stand beside Connie. "So this here's our schedule. Our map, if you like, of what we've got to do in each room…"

Chapter Six

Connie had just put the finishing touches to her light makeup following her post-shift shower when a knock came at her door. She jumped, then shook her head at her own nervousness before going over and answering it.

Lisa stood there, a smile on her face. "Hiya. I wasn't sure if you'd be here. Have you had anything to eat yet? I'm just about to go and get something. Want to come with?"

"Yes, please." Connie nodded, figuring she'd already spent several hours with the woman, so a little longer wasn't suddenly going to make them best friends. "I was heading down there myself anyway, but it'd be great to have some company. It's a little intimidating walking in there by yourself, especially when you don't know anyone, and everyone's looking at you." She grabbed her key, then switched off the light and stepped out before pulling the door closed behind her. She locked it.

The two women began walking towards the stairwell. Lisa's smile widened and she raised one eyebrow. "Yeah? From what I hear, you weren't alone at breakfast time. Sitting with Will MacIntyre, so I heard. Shockingly, he even smiled a couple of times. Though that last part could have just been a vicious rumour."

Connie gaped for a moment, then frowned. Bloody hell, she'd been told multiple times her new colleagues were friendly and helpful, but apparently nobody had thought to warn her they were also insatiable gossips! Stuffing her surprise and irritation way down low in her belly, she responded coolly, "Yes, I was. I found my way to the staff dining room, and I bumped into Will as I headed out to the kitchen. He was kind enough to escort me there, since I didn't know where I was going. What of it?" She raised her own eyebrows.

They reached the door to the stairwell, then pushed through and began descending the staircase. Holding her hands up, Lisa said, "Hey, don't shoot the messenger. I'm only telling you what I heard. It's just…" She pursed her lips thoughtfully, then went on, "Well, I guess the polite way of putting it is that he—Will, I mean—is a bit of a loner. Prefers to be by himself. Nice enough fella, when you speak to him, but he doesn't really socialise with anyone. Seems happiest traipsing around out there, mud on his boots and a spade in his hand." She jerked her head towards the nearest window. "Apparently, it's the first time he's ever willingly sat with anyone at a mealtime. Occasionally, the room gets full and there's no choice, but I hear that wasn't the case this morning."

"No, it wasn't," Connie replied dazedly, recalling the handful of empty tables. She frowned, then cleared her throat. "Well, like you say, he's a nice guy. He obviously felt sorry for me because I didn't know anyone. It's not like it was pre-planned, or we made any arrangements to repeat the experience." *No, but he did offer to give me a guided tour of the gardens—his pride and joy, by the sounds of it. And he's a loner. Doesn't socialise with anyone. Except for me, apparently. Can you even class eating breakfast together as socialising?*

They passed out of the door at the bottom of the stairs and made a left for the kitchens. "Yeah, I'm sure that's it," Lisa said, all traces of amusement now gone from her face. "He was just being polite, or whatever. Now you're getting acquainted with other folks, he'll go back to sitting by himself, glowering."

Connie shot the other woman a look. "*Glowering?* What do you mean?"

Lisa chuckled. They entered the kitchens, and she took a quick look around to see who else was there before responding. "Well, that's his thing, isn't it? The loner, looking all mean and moody. Don't think I've ever even *seen* him smile, and I've been here two years now." She shrugged, then leaned in and said quietly, "I think it's kinda hot, actually. That bad boy vibe. Don't you?" The huge grin was back. "I could just imagine him picking me up, throwing me over his shoulder and spiriting me off to an outbuilding somewhere in the grounds to have his way with me. Bet he'd be bloody good, too. Strong, rough hands. That sexy ginger beard, scratching my skin in all the right places…"

Once again left not knowing how to respond, Connie gaped. "Er…"

She was saved from having to think of anything more erudite to say by Craig's timely arrival. "Evening, ladies. Here to fill yer bellies? I've got…" Like last time, he reeled off a list of menu choices, which Connie had learned earlier were basically meals or ingredients that they had the most of for whatever reason. She understood, of course—it would never do for a paying guest to be told something was off the menu because one of the staff had eaten the last portion.

Not long afterwards, the two women were settling down to eat. The curious glances Connie had garnered that morning—which she now attributed more to her association with the apparently antisocial gardener than anything else—were now warm smiles and called-out greetings, which she returned.

"It's not quite the social hub you'd expect, this room," Lisa said, digging her fork into her mound of cottage pie. "I mean, yes, people talk in here, spend time together, but sometimes folks are just passing through quickly. You know, like this morning, you couldn't linger because you needed to eat your breakfast and get to your shift. Now, however, you've got all the time in the world. This lot," she waved her free hand around, "could be either free as birds for the evening, like you and me, or they could be mid-shift, on a break, or about to clock on. It's a twenty-four-hour operation. The hotel that never sleeps." She chuckled at her own joke. "The games and TV rooms are the place to be for socialising. You'll never find your buddy Will in there, that's for sure. God knows where he hides out when he's not working. In the attics, probably."

Connie thought she detected a hint of bitterness in her colleague's tone. Was there more to this Will's-a-loner thing than Lisa was letting on? She clearly had the hots for him. Had he rejected her at some point, and she'd never got over it?

Rather than responding—and what could she say to that, anyway?—Connie turned her attention to her own meal.

Silence reigned, then, as Lisa no longer seemed in the mood to talk, and Connie didn't want to start a conversation because of the whole not-inviting-confidences thing she'd decided on. It was so important she kept any acquaintances and friendships purely superficial. She couldn't let on to anyone that she'd run away from her old life, because that, surely, would increase the chances of it catching up to her.

It was only as she wordlessly followed Lisa back to the kitchens to return their dirty dishes that she wondered if perhaps, she wasn't the only one who'd ended up escaping to Bowdley Hall Hotel. Could *that* be why Will didn't ask any questions, even though he'd been the one to find her? Was that why he kept himself to himself? Maintained a prickly exterior so nobody would dare to get close? Or even want to try?

Of course, there was a chance he just didn't like other people very much. But he'd been so kind to her. And then there was the invite to tour the gardens which, the more she learned about him, the more she thought about it, seemed utterly out of character.

Had he made an exception for her because he sensed a kindred spirit? That they had something in common? That somehow seemed more likely than him fancying her and suddenly turning from a glowering loner into a grinning flirt.

Yes, that had to be it. She nodded decisively, then passed through the door Lisa was holding open for her with a smile. "Thanks."

They left their stuff with the potwash and hurried out again. "So, what are your plans now?" Lisa asked, her earlier moodiness apparently forgotten.

Connie shrugged. "I haven't got any, really. Why, what are you doing?"

"Games room. There's always something going on in there. Wanna come?"

"Sure. If you don't mind me tagging along." It beat going

back to her room to sit around doing nothing.

"*Pfft.* You're not tagging along. You've got as much right to be there as me. Come on, I'll introduce you to some more folks."

When they entered the games room, it was a hive of activity—a million miles away from the almost-empty room she'd encountered when Frances had first shown it to her. However, one thing remained the same: Nico and Ashley were playing pool. This time, though, there were others hanging around them, either watching for entertainment value, or waiting to play the winner.

Lights blazed, as did a big fire in the hearth. The room was bright, warm, and buzzing with energy. Connie felt her spirits lift just being here.

"Come on," Lisa said, with a wave to the gang at the pool table as they passed by, "let's see what's on TV."

Although part of Connie felt more inclined to stay in the games room, with its happy, energetic vibe, another part of her thought it would be a wiser idea to go into the TV room. There, she wouldn't be expected to talk to anyone—and if she didn't talk to anyone, she wouldn't have to answer questions, wouldn't have to tell people about herself. "Sure," she said, smiling and nodding at people as she followed Lisa towards the TV room door, "great idea."

When she turned to push the door closed behind them, she caught sight of something which made her freeze in her tracks. Across the room, Nico and Ashley both remained by the pool table, but neither of them was playing right at that second. They were staring. At her. Intently.

Gulping hard, Connie closed the door, sealing them into

darkness only broken by the flickering images from the huge screen. Her heart pounding, she scurried to take the seat beside Lisa and settled silently down to watch the TV—which was currently less than half an hour into one of her favourite films, *Mamma Mia!*

Grateful for the distraction the feel-good movie would provide, she focussed on it, and was soon absorbed in the stories of the characters on screen, all thoughts of moody gardeners, and gawping porters and waiting-on staff left far, far behind.

Chapter Seven

Everyone who'd watched *Mamma Mia!* to the end emerged into the light of the games room, rubbing their eyes and stretching, Connie included. As always, she'd thoroughly enjoyed the movie—it didn't seem to diminish, or get boring, no matter how many times she watched it. Now, though, her heart raced as she wondered what would happen next. She'd successfully managed to socialise without *actually* socialising for the last hour or so, but now, avoiding talking to people would be much more difficult. Especially since the games room appeared even busier now than it had when they'd passed through earlier.

Could she get away with slipping off to her room? Feign exhaustion following her first day on the job? Explain she was on an early shift the following morning?

Before she got the opportunity to find out, Lisa nudged her. "I think our resident Casanova is trying to get your attention." She smirked.

Connie's mouth went dry as she reluctantly looked where Lisa was pointing, already suspecting who she was going to see. *Damn it.* Her suspicions had been correct—Nico Moretti, still holding court at the pool table, was waving at her. When they made eye contact, he beckoned, his white teeth flashing as he beamed at her.

Panic making her heart race even faster, she turned to Lisa and muttered, "What the fuck am I supposed to do?"

Lisa frowned, her expression clearly saying she thought Connie was crazy. "What do you mean? Go and bloody well talk to him!"

"B-but you just said he's the resident Casanova."

"So?" Lisa gave a mischievous grin. "He just wants to talk to you, play a little pool maybe. He's not asking you to marry him and have his babies, for Christ's sake!" She put her hand on Connie's lower back and gave her a little shove in Nico's direction. "Go on. Put the poor boy out of his misery. I'm going to go and play cards with the others."

He was hardly a *boy,* in Connie's opinion, but her hesitation was starting to draw attention from others in the room, and that was the last thing she wanted. But then, she didn't want to be seen as easily led by peer pressure and a handsome face, either. Swallowing down the sigh that desperately wanted to escape, she approached the pool table, hoping she didn't look as reluctant as she felt. That would just be rude. "Hi, Nico."

His smile widened, deepening the dimples in his cheeks. He really was *very* good looking. "Connie. Good to see you again. How was your first day?"

She shot a look around the table to see who else was there. Ashley still lingered, though he no longer had the other pool cue—a tall, well-built black guy seemed to be Nico's current opposition. Ashley nodded a greeting when her gaze landed on him, and she gave a closed-mouth smile in response. She didn't know any of the others, but figured that would change soon enough. "It was fine, thanks. Lots to learn, but I'm sure I'll soon get the hang of it. I've been tagging along with Lisa. Poor woman's been lumbered with me all day, then was nice enough to let me eat dinner with her, too. She must be sick of me by now."

Nico chuckled. "I doubt anyone could ever get sick of *you*, Connie. Now, if you'll excuse me, I think it's my shot. This is Wayne, by the way." He indicated the black man. "I'm sure the others will introduce themselves while I take my go."

Ignoring his slightly sycophantic comment about nobody getting sick of her, she smiled at Wayne. "Hi. Nice to meet you. I'm Connie. I just started working here today."

He returned her smile, the action transforming what she'd first thought to be quite an ordinary face into an incredibly handsome one. "Good to meet you, too, Connie." He jerked the pool cue towards Ashley. "I think you've already met Ashley, right?" When she nodded, he indicated the only other woman at the table—a petite, very pretty brunette. "And this is Jessica."

Suddenly remembering how Nico and Ashley had been staring at her when she'd escaped into the TV room, Connie sidled closer to Jessica—strength in numbers, perhaps?—and gave her a warm smile. "Hi, Jessica. Great to meet you, too." She chuckled nervously. "I feel like a stuck record. And there are so many people working here that I'm sure I'll be repeating myself for some time to come."

Returning her grin, Jessica said, "Hi. And yeah, I think you will. So, the rumour mill has already been busy, but I'd quite like to find out direct from the source... you're the newest chambermaid, right?"

Ugh, not that bloody rumour mill again. I'm going to have to tread incredibly carefully here. She nodded. "That's right." Then, eager to turn the conversation away from herself, continued, "So, what about you? What do you do here?"

"I'm mostly on Reception, but sometimes help out with admin work, too."

"And you enjoy it?" she prompted. Anything to keep the topic of conversation from being her.

"Absolutely. I've always wanted to work in the hospitality industry, and being on Reception means I get to meet all kinds of interesting people, help them out, give them pointers and tips to make their stay even better. Plus, no two days are ever the same. I don't mind doing the admin from time to time, but I much prefer being out front, meeting our guests."

"Sounds like you're the perfect woman for the job then." *And you probably have your finger firmly on the pulse of this place, too.* Wondering if she could take advantage of that fact without having too much expected of her in return, Connie thought carefully about her next words. "Can I, uh, ask you something?" She'd lowered her voice, and hoped Jessica would get the hint that she wanted to know something a tad sensitive.

A little line appearing between her perfectly-shaped eyebrows, Jessica replied, "Yes, of course. What's up?"

"Is it, er, true that Nico is a bit of a... er, how to put it politely—"

"A player?" Jessica suggested.

"Yes. A player."

She screwed up her nose and shrugged. "Full disclosure, Wayne and I are together, so I'm out of bounds and therefore perhaps not best placed to answer the question. However, from what I've seen and heard," she glanced over to make sure he wasn't listening to their conversation, "he's less of a player and more of an insatiable flirt. Why? Do you like him?"

"*Like* him?" she squeaked, then bit her lip, hoping no one else had heard. "I only met him yesterday! I don't even know him. I just... well, it seems rumours fly around this place at a rate of knots, and I wanted to know the truth, that's all. Forewarned is forearmed, and all that." The words sounded lame even to her own ears, but since she couldn't even explain to *herself* why she cared if Nico was a player, there was no way she could explain it to someone else, was there?

Jessica nodded thoughtfully. "Yes, that's true. Sometimes it's fun to have a laugh and a joke and a spot of flirting without any intention of it leading anywhere, isn't it? There's often so much pressure, so much expectation these days, that people are scared to partake in meaningless flirting, in case their intentions are misconstrued."

Idly wondering if Jessica was a closet psychologist, or a psychic—that would explain how she'd hit the nail on the head without Connie even knowing herself what she meant—Connie nodded too. "Yes, absolutely. I'm not looking for a relationship, so it's worth knowing I can engage in a bit of banter with Nico without worrying he'll take it the wrong way." She smiled tightly. "There are so many people working here—it's a bit unnerving to be the new girl, trying to learn the ropes, both with regards to the job and my new colleagues." *Huh, so much for not divulging anything to anyone, Con. You're getting a little personal here.*

"I get it." She shrugged. "But we were all new once, so try not to worry too much. You can take most of us as you find us. Anyway," she glanced over at the pool table, where Wayne was currently bending to take a shot, "I have to use the bathroom, so I'll leave you to your flirting. Enjoy!"

Connie's mouth dropped open, but Jessica had hurried off before she could formulate a response. On the one hand, the other woman had figured out what Connie hadn't, but on the other hand, she'd assumed Connie desperately *wanted* to flirt with Nico. *Damn it.* She'd have to be careful what she said, how she behaved, otherwise the infamous rumour mill would have something else to circulate.

Desperate to extricate herself from the situation, especially now she was now no longer conversing with Jessica, the temptation to bolt became overwhelming. But she couldn't be rude and simply walk away—not only was it not in her nature, but in itself would probably get people gossiping. Pulling in what she hoped would be a calming breath, she stepped up to the pool table. The shot Wayne had taken was still playing out, the balls clacking and bouncing off each other and the sides of the table. Now was as good a time as any to make her excuses. "Enjoy the rest of your evening, guys. I'm shattered after my first day—I'm heading to bed. Goodnight."

She turned and headed for the door, their responses trailing in her wake. A glance over at the tables by the fire showed Lisa in the thick of her card game, the tip of her tongue just peeking between her lips in concentration. Connie sagged a little with relief—the other woman wouldn't even notice she'd gone, and if she was miffed about Connie not saying she was leaving, she'd use the excuse that she hadn't wanted to interrupt the game. Like seemingly everything just lately, she was probably reading too much into it anyway.

She opened the door and slipped into the corridor, struck by how much cooler it was. But then, the games room was full of warm bodies *and* had a blazing fire. Out here, it was just her. And right now, that was precisely what she wanted. She closed the door behind her with a satisfying click, happy to leave her new colleagues behind. As promised, they'd all been very nice, but she'd done quite enough people-ing for one day.

When she was almost at the stairwell leading to the staff quarters, a male voice called her name. Her heart gave an unpleasant lurch. *Oh, shit—just when I thought I'd got away with it.*

She turned, but to her surprise was faced not with Nico, but Ashley. Pasting a smile onto her face, she said, "Ashley? Everything all right?"

He walked up to her, concern etched into his handsome features. "Yes, *I'm* all right. I was just checking on *you*. You seemed to scurry off quickly there. I wanted to make sure someone hadn't upset you or anything." He raked a hand through his hair, leaving a tuft sticking up at the front which she found herself itching to smooth down, but didn't.

Forcing herself to meet his gaze, she replied, "No, I'm not upset. Honestly. I'm just…" She blew out a breath, realising she was on the verge of divulging information yet again. God, keeping people at arm's length was much harder than she'd expected it to be.

Perhaps she should ask Will for some lessons. He seemed to be the master. "It's been a long, hectic day, and I'm tired. Not really in the mood for any more socialising. All I want to do is curl up in bed with a book and read until I fall asleep—which I suspect won't take long at all tonight." Her smile was genuine this time. "But thank you for checking. It was very sweet of you."

Ashley gave a one-shouldered shrug. "I'm a sweet guy." He smiled widely, mischief glinting in his brown eyes. "You know, you should take the time to find out just *how* sweet." He waited a beat, then, realising he wasn't going to get a response out of her—or at least not the one he wanted—stepped back, his smile fading. "Well, as long as you're all right, I'll leave you to it. Goodnight, Connie."

Dully, she replied, "Goodnight, Ashley. See you around."

Apparently unperturbed by her lacklustre response, he said seriously, "I look forward to it." He spun on his heel and headed back in the direction he'd come from.

Shaking her head, Connie turned and climbed the stairs, relief seeping into her bones as every step brought her that bit closer to her room. To closing and locking the door behind her, to putting on her pyjamas, to grabbing the book she'd borrowed from the shelf in the corridor outside her room, to snuggling beneath the covers and losing herself in someone else's life. Someone else's drama. Anything to distract her from the drama that was her own life.

Christ, she had enough shit going on without other people adding to it. First her thinking Will was flirting with her—a suspicion which had had weight added to it by Lisa's comments about Will being a grumpy loner. Then the odd stares from Nico and

Ashley, followed by Nico's quip about not being able to get bored of her. And now Ashley was apparently throwing his hat into the ring, for want of a better expression. All three men were gorgeous—and the latter two seemed fully aware of the fact. But she simply wasn't interested in entanglements of any kind—how could she get that across without sounding bitchy? How did she achieve what Will seemed to have done—a reputation for keeping himself to himself, but without people disliking him? Would she, too, have to forego sitting with people at mealtimes, and using the TV and games room? Rather than just keeping people at arm's length, would she have to avoid them altogether—work hours excepting?

It was a hugely unpleasant sacrifice, but it might just be one she'd have to make in order to keep her secrets, her anonymity. To keep her past as firmly that: the past.

As she locked her bedroom door behind her, she decided it would be worth it. After all, what was worse: being a bit of a loner, or living miserably under the thumb of an abusive bully and being constantly worried about her safety? Talk about a no-brainer.

Chapter Eight

Two weeks later

With an almost overwhelming sense of relief, Connie pushed her housekeeping cart through the door into the department. That had been one *hell* of a busy day. A few days ago, she'd been deemed more than capable of working on her own, instead of tagging along with Lisa—a positive in terms of her employers apparently being pleased with her, and not having to spend each shift with Lisa while attempting to keep some distance between them, but a negative in terms of the work being harder. It was much more difficult to strip a bed then make it up with new sheets and covers by yourself than when there were two of you. But she was quickly getting the hang of it, and although she was currently much slower than the others at turning a room over, she found she actually enjoyed the work. There was a certain sense of satisfaction at freshening up a room for the guests to relax in after a busy day sightseeing in the Highlands. *And* she'd learned just how far Bowdley Hall Hotel was prepared to go to ensure the highest possible comfort and enjoyment for their guests—hence the bumper box of condoms she'd spotted in the department on her first day, which turned out to be one of many.

She was ready for some relaxation herself, now. Time to grab a quick meal, then head back to her room for a shower and some quality time with her book. She might even have a long soak in the bath, instead of a shower. It was great to have the choice—the ultra-modern theme of the bathrooms in the hotel carried through to the staff quarters, too. No expense had been spared, apparently. Smiling, she stowed her cart away and was just about to turn and head for the kitchens when Isla appeared.

"Connie?"

"Yes? Everything all right?" Oh God—had she done something wrong?

The older woman nodded. "Absolutely. You're doing great, lass—dinnae look so worried. I would let you know if there was a problem." Connie sagged a little with relief. "Anyway, the reason I called you back is because Frances has left a message. Could you go and see her in her office, please?"

Her mouth drying and her heart pounding, Connie nodded. "Yes," she croaked. "I'll head there right away."

Isla gave a kind smile. "I dinnae think you need to worry about this, either. I'm sure she's just checking in on you, to see how you're getting on."

With a half-hearted nod, Connie thanked her line manager and left the department, then headed for Frances's office. She hoped Isla was right, that Frances *was* just checking in. She couldn't think of anything she'd done wrong, anyway—and besides, Isla had literally just said she'd let her know if there was a problem, so it couldn't be anything to do with the standard of her work.

With that comforting thought in mind, she concentrated on slowing her breathing and heart rate as she made her way along the corridor. It wouldn't do to turn up to see Frances looking like she'd run a marathon. At least she could find her boss's office now—two solid weeks of working here had given her a thorough knowledge of the hotel's layout, and she hadn't got lost or even taken a wrong turning for about a week. Progress indeed.

She arrived at Frances's office and knocked on the door.

"Come in!"

After taking a final calming breath, Connie opened the door and entered. "Hi, Frances. Isla said you wanted to see me?"

The older woman smiled from her seated position behind her desk. "Connie," she said warmly. "Come and take a seat—I won't keep you too long. You're probably ready for something to eat after your shift."

Connie closed the door and did as she was told. "It's fine. What did you need to see me about?"

Despite her best attempts, either her expression or voice must have given her away, since Frances let out a chuckle. "Connie, it's nothing to worry about, I promise you. I'm told you're already working by yourself, and doing a fine job. That's great news—well done."

Having heard the words from the horse's mouth, so to speak, Connie finally relaxed. "Thank you. I'm really enjoying it, actually. I'm slower than the others, but I'm doing my best to get up to speed."

"As long as you're doing a good, thorough job, Connie, I'm happy. The speed will come with practice. At this stage, much better to get it right than to rush. Anyway, I just wanted to talk to you about a couple of things. I'll get the dullest—albeit very important—one out of the way first. Wages. It'll almost be time to start working on this month's payroll, and it occurred to me that because of the unusual circumstances of your employment here, we haven't followed the usual procedures. *Any* procedures, really." She tutted.

"Which led me to thinking… what's your status with regards to a bank account?"

Her heart sinking, Connie twisted her hands together in her lap. "I, er, had a joint account with *him*. I'd been hiding some cash away here and there for a while, taking out small amounts he wouldn't notice or would assume were just normal spending money. Then, just before I left, I took out as much as the cash machine would allow, and ditched all my cards. I knew he'd be able to track me down if I made any more withdrawals. So at the moment, I'm strictly cash only. I don't even have any ID that I can use to open an account in my name. I… shit." She ran a hand through her hair. "I thought I'd been well prepared, but I guess the truth of it is, I wasn't. I made my decision, then I ran with it, no matter the consequences. I just wanted *out,* before I cracked."

"Hey…" Frances cooed, jumping out of her seat and coming around to crouch beside Connie's. She took her hand and squeezed it, her skin warm and soft. "Don't get upset—it's not a problem. I understand why you ditched the card, the ID. It's worked for you so far, hasn't it? There's been nothing on the news, and you haven't been listed as a missing person. You're safe here. I can sort something out. Pay you in cash."

Connie sniffed and met her boss's eyes. "I'm so sorry I dumped all my problems on you. I bet you're rueing the day you met me. Wishing Will hadn't found me. Or that I *had* got hypothermia and—"

"*Hey!*" Frances snapped, squeezing Connie's hand again, harder this time. "We'll have none of that, lass, thank you very much! I *told* you from the beginning I would help you, and that's what I'm going to do—all right? You have a roof over your head, you have food in your belly, you have a job. And very soon, you'll have some wages."

"B-but won't you get into trouble? You know, because of tax and national insurance, that kind of thing?"

Her voice softer now, Frances replied, "You let me worry about that. Now," she stood and returned to her seat. "The other thing I wanted to talk to you about… How are you getting on, generally?"

Swallowing hard in an attempt to get a grip on her emotions, Connie nodded, then cleared her throat. "Excellent, thanks. Like I said, I'm really enjoying the work."

Frances stared at her in silence for a moment, then sighed, leaned forward in her chair and rested her elbows on the desk. "Connie, hen, I'm not talking about your job. We've covered that. I'm talking about everything else. Your new home, your colleagues… are you getting on with people, making friends? Settling in all right?"

"Oh, I see what you mean. Yes, everyone's very friendly and helpful. The food is great, my room is great, the facilities are fantastic. I love it here. I've even stopped getting lost!" She chuckled. "Though I've probably jinxed myself now."

To Connie's surprise, Frances dropped her head into her hands. A few wisps of red hair had come lose from her hair grip and hung down beside her fingers.

Connie gaped. "F-Frances? Are you all right?"

Frances lifted her head just enough to make eye contact. "You're quite the mistress of *not* saying things, aren't you?"

Frowning, Connie replied, "What do you mean?"

"I thought we'd established that you could trust me. And yet you're only telling me half the story—if that. I'm genuinely concerned and interested in your wellbeing, in how you're getting on, but you're only giving me the bare minimum. I *know* my employees are friendly and helpful, but have you *made friends* with any of them? Do you eat meals with anyone? Watch TV? Play cards? Use the gym, the pool? *Give* me something, lass, would you? Please? I'm not trying to pry—I just want to make sure you're happy."

"I..." A lump appeared in her throat as a realisation hit her: she was lying by omission, and being deeply unfair to this kind, caring woman in the process. She sighed. "Frances, I'm sorry. I *do* trust you. I'm just... I've got used to being evasive since I've been here, giving people the tiniest amount of information I can get away with, and I guess it stuck. I'm making friends to an extent. I'm still so scared of anyone finding out how I ended up here, about it getting out that I'm here, and then *him* finding me, that I'm keeping people at arm's length. But I'm not sitting in my room all the time—I eat meals with the others, I watch TV. I don't play cards, but that's because it's not my thing. As for the gym and the pool—well, not yet. I didn't exactly pack a swimsuit or gym kit, so I was planning on venturing out to buy some stuff once I got paid." She gave a weak smile, hoping her admissions would wipe the look of utter frustration from her boss's face.

Her hopes, however, came to nothing. The older woman's brow creased, then she closed her eyes and shook her head. *For Christ's sake, what have I said wrong now? Surely she doesn't want me going swimming in my underwear! That'd get some complaints from the guests.*

After a moment, Frances opened her eyes and met Connie's gaze. Her eyes were soft, her expression understanding. But somehow, Connie still got the sense she wouldn't like what her boss was about to say. "I get what you're saying, lass. I know you're frightened he'll find you somehow. But I don't think you're giving people much credit. I'm certainly not saying you should tell all and sundry about your situation, but I don't think you should keep folks at arm's length, either. For one, the more mysterious a person is, the less they give away, the more people want to know about them—it's human nature, especially around here. The more they'll ask questions, the more they'll dig. And I'm sure you've already worked out how quickly word gets around in this place. If you don't tell someone something soon, they'll start coming up with theories—and that could be a hundred times worse. Some of our folks have rather vivid imaginations.

"Secondly, have you stopped to think about the other impacts this could have on you? Your mental health? You're determined to leave your old life behind, which is fair enough, and completely your decision. But at the moment, you seem to be living a half-life. You haven't stepped fully into your new life, haven't embraced it. Aside from everything we've just talked about, that cannae be good for your mental wellbeing. Plus, if you don't build a new life for yourself here—or anywhere else, if you decide to move on, which I hope you don't—then he's won, hasn't he? He made your old life so miserable, so ridden with anxiety, you felt you had no choice but to walk away from it, but even now, he's managing to ruin things for you. You're not letting your guard down, not letting people in." She paused, spread her hand out, palm-side down on the desk, then slapped the surface. "Connie, you *deserve* to be happy. You've been through so much, and you've been so goddamn brave. Be brave *now*, hen. Stick two fingers up to that bullying *bastard*. He won't know it, but *you* will." She slapped the desk again, then blew out a breath. "Christ, I feel like a motivational speaker. I'm sorry, I don't know where all that came from. And I hope you don't feel I've overstepped the mark, or stuck my nose in. That wasnae my intention. I just… I care about you, lass, and want you to be happy here."

Connie remained silent, her brain whirring with everything Frances had said. She wasn't quite sure what to make of it all just yet, but the older woman had some incredibly valid points. Connie had also got, for the first time, the impression that there was a particular *reason* Frances had bent over backwards to help her, especially since she'd discovered exactly why Connie was here. Maybe she'd been through something similar herself in the past, or someone she knew had. It would certainly explain her motivational speech, her passion, her emphasis on Connie embracing her current circumstances. Regardless of the origins, it clearly meant a lot to Frances, and for that reason alone Connie had listened, and would give some serious thought to it.

She smiled. "It's all right, Frances. I don't feel you've overstepped the mark, or stuck your nose in. It's blindingly obvious that your heart is in the right place. I'm just... well, I'm messed up at the moment, aren't I? You've given me plenty of food for thought, and although I can't promise I'll suddenly become this terribly brave person, I know deep down you're right. Therefore, I *can* promise that I'll try to move forward. Try to live a full life here. Make friends. I'll have to find some way of doing that without either telling people everything or lying to them, but I'm sure I can come up with something."

Frances returned her smile. "Like I said earlier, you're the queen of *not* saying things. So all you've got to do is think about how you'll describe your backstory without giving away information you're not willing to divulge. I don't know..." She shrugged. "Perhaps say something like you had a bad break-up and wanted a fresh start. It's not a *lie,* is it? Just creative truth-telling." Her lips quirked up at the corners. "And if you put emphasis on the *bad* part, most people won't press you any further anyway. If they do, just say you don't want to talk about it."

"You make it sound so simple." She couldn't help the incredulity that had seeped into her voice.

"It is, lass. But that's because it's not my situation. I can look at it objectively. You can't. It's recent, it's raw, it's hurtful. Your emotions are probably all over the place, and that's understandable. Anyway," she lifted both hands, palms up, "I've said my piece. I apologise for bombarding you, but the happiness of my employees is paramount. You're a good worker, and I'd like you to stay here. You don't need to promise *me* a damn thing, hen. You should promise *yourself* that you'll try to move forward. And know that, no matter what happens, I'll be here for you. As a shoulder to cry on, for moral support, whatever you need. Never be afraid to ask, to knock on my door. I'm here, and as always, anything you say will be kept in complete confidence."

The lump in Connie's throat was back, and this time it felt as though it was twice the size. She gulped. Sniffed. "You know," she said, her words strangled, "I think I'll take you up on that shoulder to cry on right now."

Wordlessly, Frances leapt to her feet once again and hurried around to Connie's chair. Opened her arms.

Connie went into them eagerly, the tears falling freely now. Whatever Frances's background, her past experiences, her words had hit the spot. Smashed the spot into smithereens, in fact.

She let the tears come, the sobs. Let it all out as Frances murmured soothingly into her ear, rubbed her back. She'd carry on until she was all cried out. Until all the negativity had been wrung out of her. Hopefully it would leave her empty. Neutral. Ready to move forward, to embrace positivity and start carving out a new, happier existence for herself. She *did* deserve it, and she owed it to herself. All she could do was try.

Chapter Nine

The next morning dawned bright, which felt to Connie like a good omen. It was certainly easier to be positive when the sun was shining. Hopefully it would stay that way.

Even better, she wasn't working today. Something else which would help her to start carving out that amazing new life she owed to herself—hours to fill doing whatever she wanted to. Relaxing. Fun stuff. But what could she do? Where could she go? She hadn't been paid yet, so heading into the nearest town was out, for now at least. She'd have to find out what the nearest town *was,* and how best to get there first, as well. That would go on her to-do list for her next post-payday day off.

So, what now? Getting up, getting washed and dressed, then heading for breakfast were a given.

If she didn't find anyone in the staff dining room who wanted to hang out, perhaps she'd head to the games room. Surely there'd be someone around to play pool with, or even a board game. Hell, even watching crappy daytime TV with someone would be a step in the right direction, though it wasn't exactly what you could call socialising or making friends.

With a happy sigh, she climbed out of bed and crossed to the window. She opened the curtains, then let out a gasp as she took in the sight before her. It wasn't only bright and sunny out there, it was clear. Not a cloud in the sky, which was a stunning blue, with only a single vapour trail from an airplane marring its perfection. In fact, *everything* was stunning. The surrounding hills and mountains, the sunlight glinting off the distant loch, the grass, trees, shrubs, both near and far.

She couldn't stay inside on a day like today. It would be wrong—especially since, if the stereotypes and comments of her colleagues were to be believed, days like this didn't come around too often. She should make the most of it. Go for a hike, maybe. But she didn't know the area, didn't have a map or a compass—and look what had happened last time she'd been wandering around this neck of the woods with no idea what she was doing or where she was going.

This time her sigh was one of frustration. Here she was, trying to be positive, wanting to spend time outdoors in this glorious weather, and at this rate, the most adventurous she was going to be was reading a book in the gardens.

Just then, a dark, moving shape far below caught her eye. She squinted at it. A person walking on the grass. The shadows cast by the building currently masked the person's identity, but Connie already had her suspicions. Suspicions which were proven correct as the figure passed out of the shade and into the sunlight. It was Will, his ginger hair almost glowing in the brilliant sunshine, like flames on his head. She smiled at the sight, then a thought pinged into her brain.

What if she took Will up on his offer—or whatever the hell it had been—of a tour of the gardens? He looked as though he was dressed to work, but hopefully he'd be able to spare a few minutes to show her around, or at least point her in the right direction, tell her what she should see, where she should explore.

She shrugged. Couldn't hurt to try. The worst that could

happen would be for him to be too busy, and if that were the case, she'd just mooch around by herself. No harm done either way.

That decided, she got cleaned up and dressed in her hiking gear, tied her hair into a high ponytail, then grabbed her backpack and threw in her water bottle, which she'd ask them to fill in the kitchen—maybe with something a little more flavoursome than plain water. The rucksack already held her waterproof jacket and a hat, in case she needed them. Unlikely, given the cloudless sky, but she'd learned the hard way how brutal the weather could be here. She wasn't going to take any risks.

Half an hour later, with both a full belly and water bottle, Connie slipped out into the gardens. A middle-aged couple were taking advantage of the early morning sunshine on the patio, and she exchanged smiles and greetings with them before heading in the direction she'd seen Will go earlier. The grounds of Bowdley Hall Hotel were massive, so that was certainly no guarantee of finding him, but she had to start somewhere.

Fortunately, luck was on her side, and as she passed around the side of the building, she heard the unmistakeable sounds of digging. *Thunk. Scrape. Thunk. Scrape.* Turning her head this way and that, she ascertained the direction the noise was coming from and, hoping she was right, followed a gravel path towards a gap in an ornamental hedge. As she passed through, it grew louder. *Phew— I'm on the right track.*

She crunched along the path, passing through a rose garden—not currently at its best, but beautiful nonetheless—then another gap in a hedge. Finally, she spotted him off to one side, his big body rhythmically lifting and dropping as he dug what seemed to be incredibly hard ground. She thought he'd been wearing a long-sleeved top earlier, but now he was just in a T-shirt, so had clearly got warm already. He hadn't heard or seen her yet—probably since he was making so much noise of his own—so she continued walking until she was right opposite him. Only then did he stop what he was doing and look up at her.

Surprise flitted across his face, then was rapidly replaced by pleasure. *So much for him not smiling very often.*

He straightened, then leaned his forearms on the handle of his spade. She tried not to notice how well-muscled they were. No mean feat, given how the sun was highlighting his pale skin, like it was encouraging her to look. "Well, hello there, lass. Ye picked a grand day to be out here. Beautiful, isnae it?"

She nodded. "It sure is. As soon as I woke up and saw this gorgeous weather, I had to come outside. I was wondering… if you're not too busy, can I take you up on that offer of a garden tour?"

He lifted his eyebrows. "No' working today?"

She'd have thought her outfit made it blatantly obvious, but for all he knew she could be on shift later. "Nope. I'm free as a bird. But if you don't have time, I'll understand, and perhaps you can point me in the right direction for exploring. I don't want to go too far, though, since I don't have a map or compass yet. I don't fancy getting caught out again—I have a feeling you might not be so kind if you had to rescue me from an outbuilding for a second time."

There was a moment of silence, then Will let out a snort.

"Aye, you're right there. Only a fool doesnae learn from his or her mistakes. But ye dinnae need to worry—I'd be glad to show ye around. No time like the present."

"Are you sure? I don't want to get you into any trouble."

He lifted his spade and thrust it roughly into the ground, so it stood there on its own. "Ye willnae. I told ye before, Frances is a good boss. As long as all my work gets done, she's flexible about when I do it. Has to be, sometimes, given how wild the weather can get here. Nae chance o' me slogging away in a downpour and getting drookit!"

Connie frowned. "Getting... *what*?" She loved his sexy, melodic accent, but sometimes she didn't understand what the hell he was talking about.

Will rolled his eyes, as though she'd asked the stupidest question he'd ever heard. Maybe she had. "Ye know, drookit! Pish-wet through. Drenched. Soaked. Like ye were when I found ye."

"Oh, I see. Gotcha. I'm not very well versed in Scottish slang, Will, so you'll have to bear with me."

"Aye. I can teach ye a word or two." He winked.

Heat came to her cheeks. "I'd like that."

Their gazes met and held, ramping up the warmth in Connie's cheeks until she thought her head might explode. But, for some reason, she couldn't look away. She was like a deer frozen in headlights. And so, apparently, was Will. This time she was sure he was flirting, sure he was attracted to her. The chemistry between them was palpable.

Eventually, the murmur of voices broke them out of their odd stalemate. Will cleared his throat exaggeratedly, needlessly shoved at his spade to make sure it remained in place, then said, "Right then, lass, shall we be off?"

"Aye... I mean yes." *God, what was that all about? He's going to think you're taking the piss out of him.*

He gave her a narrow-eyed glance before marching off the flowerbed he'd been digging, stepping onto the path, then turning in the opposite direction to where she'd come from and striding away. His long legs naturally meant he'd move more quickly than she did, but he was also putting some serious effort into it.

She scurried to keep up with him, wondering what kind of bizarre tour had you walking so fast you couldn't actually see what you were supposed to be looking at, much less enjoy and admire it. Granted, now she thought about it, she *did* have an amazing view of his arse in his work trousers, but although it was incredibly nice to look at, she was sure that wasn't what he'd had in mind. "Er... do you think we could possibly slow down a bit?"

"Aye, in a minute," he threw over his shoulder without breaking stride or hesitating even a bit.

Fucking hell, I'd have been better off wandering about by myself. Or relaxing with a book somewhere. This is more like a workout than a tour.

After what probably was a minute, but felt more like five, Will stopped, but didn't turn. Instead, he waited until Connie shuffled up next to him, breathing heavily. "Bloody hell," she gasped. "What in God's name was that? I didn't see a damn thing! If that's your idea of a tour, the language barrier is worse than I thought."

Will huffed out a laugh, watching her from the corner of his eye. "Dinnae fash—that wasnae the tour. We're starting now." He lifted an arm and indicated the wide-open space before them.

"Fine. But we're going to have to go at a more… sedate pace than that."

"Nae bother. Come on then." Without another word, he took off again. He was considerably slower than he'd been before, but still not even close to what she'd call a sedate walking pace. Was he nuts? This had been his sodding idea, and now he was running her ragged. If he'd wanted to kill her, he'd have been better off leaving her wet through and freezing cold in the outbuilding all those weeks ago.

After a few more minutes' speedy walking, Will stopped next to a stream. This time, he did turn, a huge smile on his face as he faced back the way they'd come. *Christ, this bloke is an enigma.* She caught up to him, spun to face the same way he did, then waited. After a beat, she was rewarded. Finally she could rejoice in the sensation of the sun on the exposed skin of her face and hands, the feel of the breeze whipping past, toying with her long ponytail. It also delivered the smells of nature—the nice ones, fortunately—into her nostrils. Birdsong—and even some cries from what she presumed were birds of prey—provided a pleasant accompaniment to it all. She sighed happily.

"This here is the edge of the estate." He made a sweeping gesture with his left arm. "The stream behind us runs right to the base o' that mountain—or vice versa, if yer being pernickety. The base of the mountain marks the other border. On the other side of the hotel from here is a good old-fashioned fence. Then, as you know, at the end of the access drive is the road."

Connie's eyebrows had crept higher and higher as Will spoke. She knew there was a lot of open countryside in this part of the world, knew the Bowdley estate was enormous, but this was something else. The stream, bubbling merrily away behind them, stretched off way into the distance on both sides. She could see the mountain, of course, but then it was, well, a mountain. But it was a *long* way away. God, just how much of the "gardens" was Will going to show her? Maybe she should have brought a packed lunch. "Wow, that's a lot of land. How on earth do you manage it all by yourself?"

"I dinnae," he said simply, fixing her in his gaze.

She blinked, trying not to fidget as his blue eyes bored into her. "W-what do you mean? I haven't seen anyone else working in the gardens, or heard anyone mention another gardener." Glancing around at the vast area, she said, "What are you, Superman or something?"

"Obviously," he said, bending his arm and flexing his bicep in an exaggerated manner. Connie's mouth dropped open. Smiling, being funny, showing off—had the Will she'd met previously been abducted by aliens and replaced by this imposter? But then, he'd *always* smiled around her. Not *much,* granted, but certainly a great deal more than other people indicated was normal for him. And he'd been amusing, even flirted with her before—or so she'd thought. Oh Christ, this was confusing!

His smirk evaporated when she didn't react, and he took pity on her. "Nae, lass. I'm no' Superman. More's the pity. But we're all for helping each other out around here, so while I take care o' the formal gardens, and use a ride-on mower for the grass immediately surrounding the hotel, for the rest o' the land, we have a much more natural way o' doing things. Farmers galore in these parts, ye see? So we let their animals graze on the land. It's a win-win situation. We dinnae have to worry about keeping the grass short, and the farmers dinnae have to worry about their livestock overgrazing their own land. Very environmentally friendly, as they say."

Connie nodded thoughtfully. "Yes, that makes perfect sense. And now you've mentioned it, I *have* seen sheep dotted around—I just hadn't realised that they were technically on this estate." She turned her attention to the rear of the hotel, where the formal gardens stood, her brow creasing. "You still have lots to look after, though."

"Aye, I do. But I enjoy it, I'm well compensated for it, and I ken I have only to say the word and Frances will draft in some help. Havnae needed it so far, though," he said proudly, puffing out his chest.

Barely tearing her gaze from his pecs, she smiled weakly and met his eyes. "Maybe you *are* Superman, after all."

He shook his head. "Nae. Just a hard worker. All it takes is graft and common sense. Tackle it logically, look after it right, and ye will be rewarded. I'm sure ye find the same thing in yer job, too."

"Yes, I suppose so. But I'm still getting the hang of it."

"Course ye are, ye've only been here five minutes. Give it a few more weeks and ye'll be Super*woman*."

"I hope you're right."

He jerked his head, indicating she should follow him, then began walking—at a normal pace now, thankfully. "So… ye're planning to stick around then, are ye?"

She shot a look at his face, wondering if Frances had put him up to finding out her intentions. Then she remembered that Frances didn't know she and Will had even had contact bar his rescue mission. Or did she? Perhaps the rumour mill reached Frances's ears too.

But Will's expression was innocent, his tone casual, so she decided to give him the benefit of the doubt. After all, who better to start opening up to than the man who'd helped her so greatly? The man who barely spoke to anyone else, so would be highly unlikely to repeat anything she'd said anyway?

Taking a leap of faith, she said, "Yes. I am. I enjoy the job, I like the people. The atmosphere is great. And of course, it's so beautiful. Like a little slice of paradise. At this point in my life, I can't think of anywhere I'd rather be."

He turned his head to look at her then, his expression serious. "I'm very pleased to hear it, lass. I'd be mighty sad to see ye go, that's fer sure."

Chapter Ten

Connie had no idea how to respond to that, so she didn't bother, though her pulse fluttered madly.

Spots of colour appeared on Will's cheeks, and he cleared his throat. "Right then. Let's have a look around, shall we?" He took off at speed, putting some distance between them before Connie could react.

Blinking stupidly, Connie followed at a more natural pace, and was relieved when Will slowed down to let her catch up. They remained silent for a while as they headed across the dew-dampened grass in the direction of the formal gardens. Connie didn't know if Will had clammed up because he was embarrassed, or because there wasn't much to say about open parkland, which was essentially just grass and trees. Possibly both.

When they drew closer to the rear of Bowdley Hall, Will finally spoke. "This here is pretty much where my input begins. Cutting the grass, looking after hanging baskets, planters, the hedges, trees, parterres. Basically providing an attractive, tidy, relaxing space for the guests."

She smiled. "Well, you certainly do that. It's beautiful."

They continued on along the outside of a hedge, away from the hall. "Back here is my domain," he said once the hedge ended, to reveal a tall wooden fence. Will opened a gate and ushered Connie through to an area containing sheds, greenhouses, and even a small vegetable patch. They stopped, and he pointed towards the hedged-off area. "This bit's off-limits to guests. If I'm not in there, ye'll usually find me here." He smiled. "Would ye like a coffee?"

Taken aback by his out of the blue question, Connie replied, "Er, yes please."

"Come on then." He made for the largest of the sheds, Connie in tow.

Once inside, the door pulled closed behind them, it was clear this shed was Will's "office". She hadn't really thought about it before, but it made perfect sense that his job wasn't solely about the physical labour. He would, of course, have to order new plants, seeds, and tools, and have plans for what he was going to do, how he was going to lay out flowerbeds, notes of where he'd planted seeds and bulbs, and so on. It wasn't just a case of digging holes and planting things willy nilly.

"Take a seat," he said, jerking his chin towards a folding chair which rested up against the wall, beneath the structure's only window. "It's black, I'm afraid, wi' sugar. If yer desperate for milk I can fetch some from the kitchens."

Her eyes having adjusted to the relative gloom compared to outside, she shucked off her backpack, then retrieved the chair, unfolded it, and sat down. "Black's fine, thanks."

He retrieved a flask from his desk—actually a sheet of plywood sitting on two stacks of wooden crates—and poured the dark liquid out into two mugs. In the small space, the rich scent soon hit Connie's nostrils, and she found herself on the verge of salivating, eagerly awaiting the delicious taste, the inevitable hit of caffeine which would follow.

She took the mug Will offered with a smile. "Thanks."

"Nae bother." He leaned against his desk, which seemed

risky, given how precarious it looked. But maybe looks were deceiving in this case, since it held up perfectly well, in spite of Will's large, muscular frame. "If it's all right wi' ye, I thought we'd have this, then I'll show ye the formal gardens."

"Of course. That would be lovely."

He nodded, then they lapsed into silence once more as they sipped at their respective drinks. For some reason, though, it didn't feel awkward, didn't feel like the type of silence that cried out to be filled with mindless chatter. So she didn't.

After a few minutes, the coffee now doing its job of both warming her and livening her up, Will put his own mug down. "Ye done?"

"Yes, thanks. Just what I needed."

He stepped over and held out his hand. "Then let's head out."

As she passed him the mug, their fingers contacted, sending an unexpected rush of heat zipping across her skin. She snatched her hand away and stood abruptly, nearly knocking the chair over in the process. Rolling her eyes at her own idiocy, she put the chair back how she'd found it, then shouldered her rucksack. When she turned, she found Will standing right in front of her, mere inches between them. She gasped.

He frowned, but said nothing. Then, as one, they stepped towards the door. Only, in the small space, this forced them closer still. They stopped, exchanging awkward smiles. "After ye," Will said, indicating the door.

"No, after you," Connie replied with a shake of her head.

Neither of them moved. The awkwardness grew, no doubt

exacerbated by the cramped conditions. Their eyes locked. Any semblance of amusement melted away. Connie's heart skipped a beat, then began thumping furiously. She knew what was going to happen, and she couldn't decide whether she wanted it to or not. Her brain and body were so busy fighting a war that when Will moved closer still, the look in his eyes intense and questioning all at once, she didn't move a muscle.

Nor did she react when he cupped her face. Or when he leaned down, his coffee-scented breath wafting over her skin.

Only when his lips, warm and surprisingly soft, contacted hers, did she do anything. To her surprise, she reached up, fisted her hands in his hair, and kissed him back. His hair and beard were coarse against her fingers and face, but she didn't mind. In fact, it felt good. As did his mouth pressed to hers, his tongue tentatively seeking entry.

She sucked in a shaky breath through her nostrils, the scent of coffee quickly joined by a mixture of what had to be Will's shampoo or shower gel and the earthy smell of nature. Plants, soil, fresh male sweat. Her head swam with the combination, and she had to consciously lock her knees to make sure she stayed upright. Sensations she hadn't experienced in so long she'd forgotten about them assaulted her: tingles wherever he touched her, sensitivity in her nipples, a dull, thumping ache low in her abdomen, a melting heat between her legs. *Shit, this escalated quickly.*

Overwhelmed by pleasure, by need, she opened her mouth and let him in. Immediately his tongue, hot and wet, sought hers. He was an amazing kisser—confident but not cocky, firm but not forceful. She found herself giving as good as she got, and the space around them quickly filled with the sounds of snatched breaths, groans, and gasps.

She didn't know if he'd read her mind—God, she hoped that *wasn't* one of his Superman-esque powers—but just as her knees became even more jelly-like, Will scooped his free arm around her back, beneath her rucksack, and hauled her roughly towards him. Momentarily grateful for the physical support, she sagged against him, enjoying the feel of his big, hard body, and using her grip on his hair to pull his mouth harder onto hers, deepening the kiss further still.

Driven entirely by lust, Connie released Will's hair and began exploring. His broad, muscled shoulders, his firm biceps, his back, his buttocks. She cupped them, squeezed them, smiling against his mouth. A smile which dropped like a stone from her face when a thought entered her head: *I doubt this is what Frances had in mind when she said I should make a new life for myself, start letting people in.*

With a strangled sound, she jerked away from Will, then pushed roughly against his chest, putting yet more distance between them.

"Connie?" She couldn't bring herself to look at him, but the confusion in his voice was blatantly clear. "What's the matter, lass? Are ye all right? Did I do something wrong? I thought you…" He let out a gusting breath, and she finally managed to look at him, and immediately wish she hadn't. "Ye…" his brow creased, "kissed me back."

She knew precisely what he was getting at, what he was asking, but for some reason she couldn't speak. Couldn't find the words to tell him that she *had* wanted it, *had* enjoyed it, and had *most definitely* kissed him back. She might not have expected it, but she'd still thrown herself into it wholeheartedly, until her common sense had kicked in. *I can't do this. I can move forward in other ways, making friends, socialising. But I can't get… involved with someone romantically. It's just too much. I'm not ready.*

Unable to articulate any of that, Connie gaped at Will. The pain and confusion in his eyes stabbed her right in the gut. She bit her lip, shaking her head. Not only was she not ready, she was unwilling to drag anyone into the mess that was her head right now. It wouldn't be fair. Will was a nice guy, he didn't deserve to be towed along in the wake of her passing from her old life to her new one. Until she could stand on her own two feet, confident that she was back in control, romance was completely out of the question.

"Will," she finally said, her voice teetering on the very edge of breaking, "I'm sorry. I really am. You didn't do anything wrong, and yes, I kissed you back. But I shouldn't have. I shouldn't have allowed that to happen. I'm… messed up. Confused. The circumstances of my being here, of you finding me…" She swallowed hard, forced herself to carry on. "I had a bad break-up, and I just can't afford to get involved with anyone else. If I led you on, I apologise. I do like you, Will, but there's no way I'm in the right headspace for this. Whatever *this* is."

Understanding had dawned on his face as she spoke, and now he gave her a tight smile, one that didn't reach his eyes. "So what yer saying is, it's not me, it's ye? That old chestnut?"

"Yes, that's precisely it. I really am sorry. I hope you can find it in your heart to forgive me. It really wasn't my intention to mess you around, or upset you. You've been very kind to me, and I hope we can still be friends." She wanted to add *and that you'll give me another chance when I've got my shit sorted out,* but didn't. How could she expect him to hang around waiting for something that might never happen?

He closed his eyes for a moment, as though thinking, and ran a hand through his hair. Connie forced away the memory of how that hair had felt clutched in her fists as they'd kissed. Thinking about what they'd just done was the last thing she should be doing, particularly since she'd resolved it could never happen again—or at least not for a very long time. If he was even still interested then. She was so screwed up she could be approaching retirement age before the mere thought of a new relationship didn't strike fear into her heart. "Aye," he said, meeting her gaze, his eyes flat and emotionless now. "It's all right. I understand. We can still be friends, lass. Just give me a few days to get *me* head straight, and we can finish this tour then, if you like."

Damn it. He was willing to stay friends, but was essentially telling her to bugger off and leave him alone for a few days. Not that she could blame him.

"Yes. Thank you," she replied in a small voice, feeling like the shittiest person ever. She didn't deserve his understanding. An overwhelming urge to hug him took hold, but she didn't succumb to it. After what had just happened, physical contact was the worst thing she could do. She didn't want to give Will mixed signals, even though, deep down, she knew if he grabbed her now, kissed her again, she wouldn't be able to put a stop to it. Wouldn't *want* to. And if they kissed a second time, especially so soon after the first, how far would it go? Would they be testing out just how sturdy that desk was?

Goddamn it! I wish I'd gone to the TV room, after all. Even the crappiest of crappy daytime TV would have been less painful than this.

"Right." She cleared her throat. "I'll, er, leave you to it. Thanks for the tour and the coffee." Her cheeks blazed as she once again remembered what that coffee had led to. *Stop it! Stop torturing yourself!* "I'll… see you around. Sorry again." She mumbled the last part, then darted for the door.

This time there was no close proximity, no awkwardness. Will remained frozen to the spot as she threw open the door and all but fell out of it. Too much of a coward to see the expression on his face, she didn't bother to turn and close the door behind her. She left it swinging gently in the breeze as she scurried towards the gate leading to the formal gardens. A moment later, she heard it shut firmly, and cringed. Despite her apologies, her partial explanation for her behaviour, his declaration that he understood, it was obvious she'd hurt him.

A sick feeling pervaded her stomach, and she prayed she wouldn't bump into anyone before reaching the safety of her room. She hurried along the gravel path, her gut lurching as she passed Will's spade still jammed into the earth, a wood and metal reminder of what a terrible person she was, of how horribly she'd treated its owner.

By the time she slumped against the back of her closed bedroom door, hot tears streamed down her cheeks.

Bloody hell, if this is me carving out a new life, perhaps the old one wasn't as bad as I thought.

Chapter Eleven

Her plans to make the most of the beautiful day gone completely out the window—along with her positive mood—Connie locked her door, dumped her backpack, then dropped heavily onto her bed, which creaked loudly in protest. She buried her face into her pillow and let the tears come. Christ, what a mess. All she'd wanted to do was get away from *him,* get away from the intense misery he'd caused. She'd achieved that, but in turn all she seemed to be doing was making other people miserable instead. Her mother, though they weren't exactly close, would probably be wondering where she was, and worrying, despite the letter she'd sent assuring her she was taking some time out and was perfectly fine. Her ex-colleagues, her friends, the rest of her family, would be confused and hurt at her taking off without a word. And now Will, who'd been nothing but nice to her, and she'd thrown it all back in his face.

She must have cried herself to sleep, because the next thing she knew, someone was knocking on her door. Rolling over, she grimaced as her muscles protested—she'd slept in the position she'd collapsed into, and her body *really* wasn't happy about it.

"Connie! Are you there? It's Lisa."

Oh God, that was all she needed. The second Lisa caught sight of Connie's face she'd know something was wrong. And she wouldn't swallow any old excuse—she was way too savvy for that. "Yeah!" she called out, hauling herself off the bed with a wince and shuffling nearer to the door. "I'm here. I just woke up. Give me a minute, I desperately need to use the bathroom."

There was a second of hesitation, a second in which Connie

suspected Lisa was pulling a confused face on the other side of the door, then, "Er, all right. I'll just… wait here then."

Willing her stiff legs to work faster, Connie went into the bathroom and closed the door. There, she used the toilet before flushing and moving over to the sink to wash her hands. She stared intently downwards as she swished and scrubbed the soap over her hands, then rinsed them under the tap, before switching it off. Only then was she brave enough to turn her attention to the mirror.

A groan escaped her lips. It was just as bad as she'd thought it would be—maybe worse. Her hair was a mess, the ponytail now wonky and strands escaping the hair tie and sticking out every which way. Her face was deathly pale, with the exception of a patch of redness between her nose and top lip. Her eyes were swollen, red and bloodshot. She might as well have a tattoo on her forehead saying *I've been crying.*

Bollocks. Now Lisa knew she was in here, there was no way she'd leave without seeing Connie. Quickly, Connie cranked the mixer tap to the coldest setting and turned it on again. Then she grabbed her washcloth and held it under the flow until it was good and soaked. That done, she switched off the water, squeezed the excess liquid from the washcloth, then folded it into an oblong, which she slapped over her closed eyes before gently pressing it flush against her skin. The chill was soothing, and she mentally crossed her fingers that it would take down the swelling, at the very least.

As she stood there, painfully aware Lisa was still waiting outside her bedroom door and would demand an explanation, she thought hard. What could she say? She couldn't tell her the truth—she might have promised she'd start to let people in, but given Lisa clearly had a thing for Will, it wouldn't go down too well. Lisa might not have any kind of claim on the gorgeous gardener, but it wouldn't exactly do their budding friendship any favours if Connie admitted not only to kissing the man Lisa fancied, but also to rejecting him afterwards.

She groaned again. Was it really a lie if she was doing it purely to protect someone? Would it be classed as a white lie if she claimed she had bad period pains? Along with a headache, perhaps?

Figuring she had no choice, she removed the cloth from her eyes and dropped it onto the edge of the sink. Then she turned on the cold water again, bent to scoop some up in her hands, and splashed her face.

She straightened, then dared another look in the mirror. Sighed. It was a slight improvement, and it would have to do. If she dallied much longer, Lisa would start banging on the door. Pulling in a deep breath, she left the bathroom and crossed over to the door. Unlocked and opened it. Lisa was still there, looking decidedly disgruntled. She unfolded her arms and said, "Oh, *finally*. I thought—" She caught sight of Connie's face and gasped. "Oh my God, what's the matter?" Without waiting for an invite, she hurried into the room and closed the door behind her, then grabbed Connie's hand and led her over to the bed. They sat down on the end of it. "Well? Tell me, please!" She squeezed Connie's hand.

Connie forced a smile. "It's no biggie. Just period pains and a headache. Bloody typical that they'd kick in on my day off, isn't it?"

It was then Lisa appeared to take in Connie's attire, including the walking boots she still wore, which Connie now saw had shed some flecks of mud and blades of grass on the carpet. Oops—she'd probably left a trail right through the building. Lisa frowned. "You've... been outside?"

"Yes. I woke up and saw how glorious the weather was so decided to go out and make the most of it. But after a while I started feeling crap, so I headed back. I just collapsed onto the bed and conked out. I was out for the count."

"Oh." Lisa dropped her gaze to their linked hands. "I'm sorry, sweetie." Then she brightened and looked up. "Are you feeling better now you've had some sleep?"

"A little." She narrowed her eyes, it suddenly occurring to her to wonder why Lisa had been knocking on her door in the first place. "Why? Oh, don't tell me someone else is sick and I'm needed in work?" She sagged. She might not really have period pains or a headache, but nor did she particularly have the energy or inclination to put in a shift.

"Oh no, nothing like that! The reason I'm here is because it's Nico's birthday, and we're having a bit of a celebration for him in the games room tonight. Obviously it's open to everyone, so no invites needed, but I know you often chill out in your room of an evening and I didn't want you to miss out." She paused, and shot Connie a sly smile. "I'm sure he'd be *delighted* to have you there."

Connie pulled her hand from Lisa's and shot her a glare. "Oh no... not this."

Lisa had the gall to look shocked. "What? What are you

talking about?"

"I was considering coming to the party, and then you had to go and say *that*. If you're determined to use the evening as an opportunity to play matchmaker, then count me out. I'm not interested."

"In Nico? Or men in general?"

"The latter."

"I see." She fell silent for a moment, and peered thoughtfully at her hands, now clasped in her lap. Then she said, "You know, I've had my suspicions about Collette…"

With a frown, Connie replied, "Suspicions? What suspicions? And what the hell has Collette got to do with anything?" Suddenly, the realisation smacked her around the head. "Fucking hell, Lisa! I'm not a lesbian! Just to be clear, there's nothing *wrong* with being a lesbian, but I don't swing that way. I definitely like men—I'm just off them for the foreseeable future."

And just like that, she'd backed herself into a corner. But it was too late to do anything about it.

Her eyes widening, Lisa said, "Any particular reason?"

Connie barely stifled a sigh. "Yes, of course. But I don't really want to discuss it. Can I just say I had a very bad break-up and leave it at that? It's pretty recent, and painful, okay? So I'm definitely not looking for romance right now."

A Cheshire cat-like grin taking over her face, Lisa replied, "Who said anything about *romance*?"

When Connie's only response was a sigh she hadn't bothered to stifle this time, Lisa went on, "Look, I understand what you're saying about your break-up. And I'm sorry to hear about it. If you *do* decide you want to talk, I just want you know I'll listen if you need me to, okay?" Connie nodded. "Good. Now, what would be wrong with just having a little fun with Nico? You're both adults."

"Why are you so struck on Nico?" she replied, frowning. "Is he the only eligible bachelor around here, or something?"

"No. Not by any means. But he seems incredibly keen on you. And he's good looking. And, despite his flirtatious nature, he's really nice, too."

Vaguely wondering what had been said behind her back for Lisa to believe Nico was 'incredibly keen', she shot back, "Ashley's really nice. Will's really nice." She knew perfectly well where Lisa was going with this, and *having a little fun* would, she supposed, be a good way of taking her mind off what had happened, and definitely counted as moving forward. She reckoned she could keep some emotional distance if she were merely having casual sex.

"So why don't you date all three of them, then?"

"Date all three...?" It was then she remembered her throwaway comment. But despite the fact she'd only been trying to deflect attention from Nico by mentioning the other two men, it seemed Lisa had latched on to it.

"Nico. Ashley. *Will.*" There was no mistaking the emphasis on the last name, and Connie's heart sunk.

Shit. I'm skating on thin ice, here. The implications of where their conversation was headed sinking in, she replied, "I can't date three men! It would be…" What *would* it be? Fun? Exciting? Light-hearted? Exhilarating? Sexy?

Downright dangerous, more like.

"Why not?" Lisa arched an eyebrow. "This is 2019, *darling,*" she drawled exaggeratedly. "I'm assuming there's a reason you mentioned those two other names, in particular? Oh, don't worry," she added, when Connie's mouth dropped open, "I *know* Will's not interested in me. He never has been, sadly. But you should totally go for it."

"You honestly wouldn't mind?" The words were out before Connie realised saying them was essentially admitting there was something between the two of them.

"*Honestly.* Cross my heart and hope to die. I've accepted I'll have to look further afield for the man of my dreams. Or even just a decent shag, for that matter." She sighed wistfully. "We could do with some fresh blood in here. It's all right for *you,*" she leaned over and nudged Connie with her shoulder, "*you're* the fresh blood. You've got your pick of the hotties. And you know… those three are *seriously* hot. A brunette, a blond, a ginger. Like the male version of *Charlie's Angels.*" She snorted and nudged Connie again.

This time Connie nudged her back, laughing too. "I suppose they are. I hadn't thought about it." Her smile faded, and she looked Lisa in the eye. "I really *hadn't* thought about it, you know. Like I said, I'm off men. And Will's so… enigmatic. Nico's an infamous flirt. And I hardly know Ashley. Hardly know any of them, actually."

"You don't need to know them. That's the whole idea of dating, remember? You spend time with someone, talk, learn about them. If there's chemistry, then *bam,* raid the condom stash in the housekeeping department and go for your life!"

Connie clapped a hand over her mouth, giggling. "You're *outrageous*."

"What?" She adopted an innocent expression. "I'm just saying… the condoms are there to be used, right? Better we take advantage every now and then than go without."

"Go without condoms? Or sex?"

"Both!" Lisa let out a sound that could only be described as a cackle.

For some reason, it hit Connie right in the funny bone and a similar cackle leapt out of her mouth of its own accord. That was it, then. They collapsed into fits of laughter, setting each other off again and again as their eyes met. Before long, tears—definitely the good kind—poured down Connie's cheeks, and she was clutching her belly—which really *was* aching now. Served her right for making stuff up.

Eventually, exhaustion forced them to calm down. "Oh, shit," Lisa gasped, wiping her eyes. "I can't remember the last time I laughed that hard, or for that long." She examined Connie's face. "I bet you can't, either."

Connie shook her head, wondering if the other woman was always this shrewd.

"You look better, though, chick," Lisa continued, her expression serious now. "Are you *feeling* better?"

She thought about it. "Yes, I am actually. They often say laughter is the best medicine, don't they?"

"I think they say that about sex, too. Oh," she slapped her

knee, "but you can't do that right now, because of your period, so the laughter will have to do until you can get your hands on one of those men. Or all three." Her eyes went round as something occurred to her. "Oh my God—all three *at once*! A foursome—what would *that* be like?"

A second wave of giggles overtook them then, and it was some minutes before they could speak again. Connie got in first, a sobering thought having loosened her lips. "They're not going to like it, though, are they? They might not even be up for it. Dating me, I mean. Much less if they know I want to see all three of them. And let's not even go there with the shagging them all at once idea! I'm not sure I could handle that, in any case."

Smiling widely, Lisa replied with a lazy lift of one shoulder, "Only one way to find out, isn't there? *Go on*! YOLO."

Connie wrinkled her nose in confusion for a moment before recalling what the acronym stood for. YOLO—you only live once. It had been yet another of her gran's sayings, one she'd frequently and vehemently thrown out there, in relation to any number of situations. She wasn't sure the old woman would have used it in *this* particular scenario—which, had she still been around and heard about it, would probably have given her a heart attack—but it didn't make the sentiment any less true.

Chapter Twelve

Later that day when Lisa knocked on her door, unlike the last time it had happened, Connie was fully prepared. Following a lengthy and heated discussion about outfits, which had resulted in Lisa scurrying off, only to return with vast armfuls of clothing for Connie to try on, Connie had showered, scrubbed, plucked, shaved, moisturised and painted. She now walked on slightly wobbly legs—due to the black patent skyscraper heels hastily borrowed from one of the waitresses—to the door, and opened it.

Lisa's jaw practically hit the carpet. "My God, girl," she said, once more striding into the room without an invite. Connie closed the door behind her. "Look at *you*." She took in Connie's artfully pinned-up hair, her carefully applied makeup, her polished finger and toenails. And, of course, The Dress—which Connie had chosen from the mound Lisa had brought with her based purely on the colour. "You'll have those men eating out of your hand."

Connie blushed and tugged at the hem of the plum-coloured garment. "Are you sure it's not too short? I mean, I love it, I really do, but I don't want to look stupid."

"Are you kidding?" Lisa gave her an incredulous look. "With legs like that, you *should* be showing them off! It's practically a public duty. And besides, there's a lot of leg, but no cleavage, so you're all good—you know you shouldn't show off both at once. Seriously, you look gorgeous. Sexy, but classy."

She bit her lip, unused to such compliments. "Thank you. So do you."

Lisa plucked at one of the spaghetti straps of her slinky black dress. "What, in this old thing?" She winked. "I don't have legs like yours, so I *am* showing off my cleavage."

With a chuckle, Connie replied, "So who are you trying to impress, then? I thought you said there was no one here you were interested in."

"I did. But you're forgetting one very important thing." Lisa wagged an authoritative finger.

"I am?"

"It's a *party.* Everyone's invited—not just people who work here. Which means plus ones, plus twos, whatever. Friends, brothers… you get the idea. There could be some fresh blood!"

Connie sniggered. "No wonder you're so hyper."

"Oh, shush, you. Now, are you ready?"

"Er, yes, I think so." She smoothed her hands down her borrowed dress, the velvety material lush beneath her fingers.

"Good. We'll head down in a minute. But first…" She reached into the silver sequinned clutch bag she held and produced a hip flask. "A little something to get us warmed up."

Connie's eyes widened. "Hey, I said I'd go to the party. And… all the other stuff. But I didn't say I'd get blind drunk."

Lisa scrunched up her face. "*Pfft.* From this tiny amount? Besides, you're only having half of it, you cheeky cow." She raised the flask. "Cheers!" She put the bottle to her lips and tipped her head back, letting the liquid pour into her mouth. Once done, she handed it to Connie. "Go on, finish it."

"What is it, anyway?" Connie sniffed tentatively at the neck of the flask. The lack of any discernible scent answered her question just before Lisa did.

"Vodka. Lidl's finest. Bottoms up!"

Rolling her eyes, Connie took a sip. It had been a while since she'd had any alcohol, so she wasn't sure how she'd react. But she *had* had a decent meal earlier, so certainly wasn't drinking on an empty stomach. Besides, the flask *was* actually tiny—it had to be, to fit into Lisa's little bag—and Lisa had probably drunk way over half the contents, so Connie decided to throw caution to the wind. *Sod it.*

Lisa let out a whoop as Connie downed the remainder of the vodka—thankfully, there really wasn't very much left—then took the flask when Connie was done with it. "Good girl. Right, just one more tiny thing… where's *your* bag?"

Sucking in a breath through her nostrils as the alcohol burn hit her throat and travelled down her gullet, Connie retrieved the black clutch bag that matched her shoes and waved it at Lisa.

"Give it here." Lisa snatched it, then removed a large handful of condoms from her silver clutch—which Connie was now beginning to suspect was actually Mary Poppins's carpet bag in disguise—and transferred them to Connie's. She obviously forgotten about Connie's made-up period. She clicked the clasp closed, then looked up at Connie, grinning widely as she handed her the bag. "There. Got you covered for all eventualities. Multiple shags with one man, or fewer shags with more men. Oh, you know what I mean!" She wafted a nonchalant hand in the air, apparently not noticing Connie's stunned expression. Either that or ignoring it. "Let's go!"

Connie, still shocked by her friend's—yes, she was definitely classing her as a friend now, something that scared and pleased her in equal measure—behaviour, silently switched off the lights and followed her from the room, then closed and locked the door.

"Come on!" Lisa grumbled as Connie trailed behind.

"I can't go any bloody faster. I haven't worn heels in forever, and it's hard to walk when the points keep sinking into the carpet. I'm scared I'm going to fall over."

Lisa waited for Connie to catch up, then linked her arm through Connie's. "There. How's that?"

"Much better, thanks. But you can't cling to my arm all night, can you? People will think we're Siamese twins."

With a snigger, Lisa said, "And I wouldn't want to cock-block you, either."

"I'm beginning to think you're obsessed with sex."

"Only because I'm not bloody getting any. But you never know, that might change tonight." She held up her free hand, her index and middle fingers crossed.

Connie mirrored the action. "Fingers crossed."

They shared a smile, then didn't speak again until they'd successfully got down the stairs to the ground floor. Connie let out a sigh of relief. "Thank God for that. I had visions of breaking my neck!"

Lisa smirked. "You could have just taken the shoes off, if you were that worried."

"I never thought of that." Connie snorted. "What an idiot. Still, if I can tackle multiple flights of stairs in these things, I should be ready for anything."

"What, like a threesome?"

Connie roughly squeezed Lisa's arm between her elbow and her side. "For God's sake, will you shut up about that? If anyone overhears you, I'll bloody throttle you. Then I'll go back to my room—*by myself.*"

Lisa's response was to make a zipping-her-mouth-closed action. She was still smiling, though, and Connie couldn't help but smile back, even while shaking her head.

By some miracle, Lisa kept quiet all the way to the games room, which gave Connie a little time to gather her thoughts. Deep down, she was glad Lisa had persuaded her to come to the party—not because of anything to do with Nico and Ashley; just in general. As Frances had correctly guessed, whenever Connie's past came up, the mention of a bad break-up seemed to be enough to stop people asking any further questions. It had worked on Will and Lisa at any rate—and as Connie had discovered more and more in the past couple of weeks, Lisa was pretty damn nosey.

Connie's biggest fear had been vanquished, so she felt much happier and more comfortable about socialising now. She'd have a couple of drinks, but had no intention of getting anywhere close to drunk, so she didn't need to worry about saying something stupid while under the influence of alcohol. All she had to think about was having fun. And that was precisely what she planned to do.

As they approached the games room door, it was clear the party had already started. Music thumped out, mingled with the sounds of laughter and chatter. Connie smiled and turned to Lisa, who finally spoke. "Ready?"

Connie gave a decisive nod. "Ready."

"Then let's go." She opened the door, and they entered the room.

As they walked across the carpet, the thudding base vibrated up through Connie's feet and into her entire body. God, she wouldn't have to even bother about trying to hold a conversation with this much noise going on.

Lisa nudged her. "Look—there's the birthday boy!"

Connie turned her attention to where her friend was pointing. The pool table had been shifted to one side of the room to provide space for dancing, and he was leaning against it, a bottle of something in his hand and a smile on his face. Surrounding him were the usual suspects—Ashley, Wayne, and Jessica—as well as a few people Connie didn't recognise. It couldn't be anyone from the hotel—she at least *recognised* everyone now, even if she hadn't yet learned or remembered all of their names. "And he's got some people with him who don't work here, just like you said. Fresh blood."

Eyes gleaming, Lisa gave an almost-maniacal smile. "And it's not even *my* birthday. Come on, let's go and say hello."

Without waiting for a response, Lisa all but dragged Connie over to the group. "Hi," she trilled, loud enough to make herself heard. "Happy birthday, Nico!" She released Connie's arm, then moved in to give him a friendly peck on the cheek while Connie politely smiled hello to everyone else.

"Thank you." He shifted his gaze to Connie, his eyes lighting up. "You made it. You look stunning."

Casting her sudden shyness to one side, she ignored his comment and copied what her friend had done, pressing a kiss to his cheek. A delicious spicy cologne invaded her nostrils, with an undertone of shampoo. "Happy birthday!" Then, stepping back, she added, "Nice badge."

He looked down at the gaudy badge pinned to his shirt pocket, which read *Old Man*. Shaking his head, he jerked a thumb in Ashley's direction. "This twat's idea of a joke."

Ashley, having overheard them, shrugged. "What can I say, mate? I saw it and thought of you."

Nico elbowed him, then said, "Drink, ladies?" He indicated the array of cans and bottles behind him on the pool table.

"Sure," Lisa said. "What's on offer?"

He put down his own drink—beer, Connie noticed—and turned to look. "Beer, cider, alcopops, schnapps. And I think there's a bottle of vodka knocking around somewhere. Though if you want something else, I can go and buy it from the bar."

"No, no, there's no need for that," Lisa replied. "A WKD is fine by me."

With a nod, he retrieved a bottle of lurid blue liquid, used a conveniently-placed opener to pop off the lid, and handed it to Lisa, who murmured her thanks. "And for you, Connie?"

"I'll have the same, please."

"Coming up." He repeated the action, but this time, when he'd handed over the drink, he retrieved his beer and gently clinked the bottle against Connie's. "*Salute.*"

"*Salute.*" Her pulse skipped as their eyes met and held, and butterflies invaded her tummy as she contemplated the evening ahead, and what it might hold. She glanced over at Ashley, to find him watching the two of them. Was *he* wondering whether she and Nico were going to get it together tonight? Or was he hoping they wouldn't?

The more Connie thought about it, though, the more she realised Ashley didn't appear jealous—merely interested. Perhaps she'd got it wrong before—perhaps Ashley *wasn't* attracted to her. Or maybe he'd decided to step aside and let his friend make a play for her. Ugh, so many perhapses, so many maybes, so many what ifs. She was overthinking again.

Luckily, Lisa's voice snapped her out of it. "So, Nico, I see we've got some outsiders in our midst! Are you going to introduce me?"

"Of course," he said smoothly, giving Connie a regret-filled smile before turning to do as he'd been asked.

She took a sip of her drink and stood in the periphery, smiling and nodding at the relevant moments as Nico introduced the three women and two men—who turned out to be relations or good friends of various Bowdley employees. Both men were tall and good looking, and she hoped Lisa got her wish and would hook up with one of them tonight. Maybe both—after all, if Connie was being encouraged to try a threesome, why shouldn't Lisa give it a go, too?

Smiling to herself, she took another sip of her drink. Just then, Nico appeared at her side. "Something funny?"

Swallowing quickly, she replied, "N-nothing important. So… great party." A thought occurred to her. "And Frances is okay with this?"

He nodded, then swigged his beer. "Yeah. We have parties like this from time to time, and she's fine with it. We always ask permission, first, though. The good thing about this room is it's so far from the guest bedrooms and public areas that the music would have to be way louder than this for any of the guests to hear. Basically, as long as paying guests don't hear the music, or us, or see us behaving in an," he lifted his fingers into air quotes, "'unbecoming manner', then it's all good."

"So vomiting in the swimming pool is out, then?" Connie said with a smirk. Out of the corner of her eye, she saw the majority of the group moving off towards the 'dance floor', leaving Lisa with the two handsome newcomers, and Connie with Nico and Ashley. Her stomach flipped, the butterflies acting up again, and she took another swallow of her WKD.

Nico's eyes glinted with amusement. "Yes, I'm afraid vomiting in the swimming pool is *definitely* out."

"Shame," Connie replied, deadpan. "It's on my bucket list and everything."

Nico and Ashley sniggered, leaving Connie feeling very pleased with herself. She was actually doing okay—enjoying herself, even.

Then Ashley piped up, "There's always streaking in the formal gardens, if you're looking to do something wild. The hedges are so high the guests can't see in, even from the top-floor bedrooms."

Nico shot his friend a dirty look and nudged him so hard he

almost dropped his drink. "What?" Ashley's eyes widened, then a look of realisation swept over his face. "Oh shit, sorry. I totally forgot."

Connie frowned as the two men exchanged meaningful eye contact, apparently attempting to communicate without using words. She cleared her throat. "Excuse me—what is going on?"

"*Nothing*," they said together, turning to her, their faces the very picture of innocence.

She didn't buy it for a second. "Bullshit. *You,*" she looked at Ashley, "mentioned the formal gardens, and then *you,*" she turned her gaze on Nico, "desperately tried to shut him up. So, is there something I should know?"

Both men shuffled awkwardly, dropping their gazes to the floor, then back up to her.

Connie raised her eyebrows expectantly. "Well?"

They looked at each other, and Nico nodded before turning to Connie with a sheepish grin. "We, er… we heard something. About you. And Will."

Chapter Thirteen

Connie's heart thundered, and she flushed. *Of course you bloody well have.* Part of her itched to hotfoot it back to her room, and bollocks to the rumour mill. But a bigger part was eager to know what had been said—at least she could give her own version of events if what Nico and Ashley had heard turned out to be a load of crap.

With a coolness that certainly wasn't reflected on the inside, she replied, "Oh? And what might that be, then?"

Nico opened his mouth to respond, but before he spoke, Ashley tapped his arm. "Er, mate?"

"Yeah?"

Ashley gave a subtle nod towards Lisa and her new friends. "Do you think we should discuss this somewhere more private? And where we don't have to shout."

Understanding dawning on his face, Nico replied, "Good idea. Connie?" He held out his arm for her to take.

As she stared at it, momentarily frozen in indecision, a frantic movement caught her eye. She glanced over to find Lisa waving her hand down by her side, clearly to get her attention without drawing everyone else's. When their eyes met, Lisa flashed her a huge smile, then mouthed exaggeratedly, "YOLO." Then she jerked her head towards the door and nodded encouragingly.

Obviously Lisa had got the wrong end of the stick—this was a discussion, not a seduction, but there was no way Connie could convey that to her friend without words. So she simply smiled back, took Nico's arm and allowed him to lead her from the room, with

Ashley following close behind.

The moment they were out in the relative quiet of the corridor, the door closed behind them, Connie pulled her arm from Nico's and wheeled on the two men. "Come on then, what's this all about?"

Her words had come out sounding harsher than she'd intended, and both men recoiled. "Hey," Nico said, holding up his free hand—all three of them still clutched their bottles of drink, "don't get upset, please. It's nothing horrible. Just that you were seen out in the grounds with Will and apparently you looked quite… *friendly.*" He paused, grimaced, then went on, "I was gutted, to be honest. I thought I'd missed my chance."

"Your chance?" Connie arched an eyebrow. She idly wondered why Ashley was even a part of this conversation, but decided not to say anything since she didn't actually want him to leave. The more consideration she'd given the dating-three-men thing, the more the idea appealed. And if two of them were right here… who knew how the evening might turn out?

"Yeah…" Nico scrunched his mouth thoughtfully, and Connie realised she'd never seen him look so unsure of himself. She'd grown so used to the smooth, confident flirt that anything else seemed… odd. He gulped down the rest of his beer, wiped the back of his hand across his mouth, and, seemingly bolstered, continued. "I've been building up to asking you out on a date, was even planning to do it tonight, if you showed. But then when we heard you and Will might be an item… well, it kinda took the wind out of my sails."

"Will and I aren't an item," she replied.

"You're not?" Nico's eyes widened.

"No." Connie drained her own bottle, buying herself a moment to screw up her courage. This was her moment, right here, and she had to grab it firmly with both hands. A vision of Lisa's grinning face, mouthing 'YOLO' floated into her head. *Now or never. Moving forward.* Before a dozen more clichés could crowd her brain, she said, "We had a moment, yes, but that's it."

Nico frowned. "So… there *is* something between you? An attraction? You're just not actually seeing each other."

Connie lifted one shoulder in a shrug. "Something like that."

He scratched his head. "I'm confused. Just for the sake of clarity, am I too late to ask you out, or not?"

"Not at all." Blood rushed in her ears as she contemplated her next words. God, was she really doing this? Apparently so. "Casual dating suits me just fine."

"C-casual dating? You mean… non-exclusive?"

Out of the corner of her eye, Connie saw Ashley straighten. *That* had certainly got his attention. "Yeah, why not? As long as everyone's on the same page, and no one's getting hurt, I don't see a problem with it. Do you?"

He narrowed his eyes. "Before I answer that, what *is* this page, exactly? At the minute, I'm not sure I'm even reading the same book."

"To be frank, I like Will, and I like you, Nico. *And* Ashley." The two men exchanged yet another glance, Ashley's expression triumphant. "I've felt a spark with all three of you, so the ideal scenario from my perspective would be to *see* all three of you. I recently had a messy break-up, so I'm not looking for anything serious. I also don't want to have to choose between you, so this seems like the obvious solution."

That was it—she'd laid her cards on the table, and now the words had left her lips, her mouth went dry as she waited for their response.

Ashley burst out with, "I'm all for it, personally."

She stared at him for a moment, taking in his ear to ear grin and the sparkle in his eyes. Then she turned her gaze on Nico, who was nodding slowly.

"Ye-ah…" he eventually said, looking from Connie to Ashley, then back again. "I don't see why not. It's unorthodox, but as long as everyone's happy, and we keep lines of communication open to ensure everyone *stays* happy, then I think it's a great idea. Better to date you non-exclusively than not at all." He paused, then his thoughtful expression turned wicked. "Does that, er, mean a threesome could be on the cards? With me and Ash, I mean. Not sure I'd be comfortable with Will. Though never say never. If you'd have asked me ten minutes ago if I'd be happy sharing a beautiful woman with two other blokes, I'd probably have said no way, and now look where we are."

Connie's brain was a maelstrom of thoughts and emotions. She could scarcely believe what was happening. Had she passed through into some kind of parallel universe when she'd crossed the England-Scotland border? A universe where men, rather than being possessive, controlling, and volatile, were open-minded, and happy to share women? Either way, she was going to embrace it—starting right now. "You like the idea of a threesome, do you?" she asked Nico. "With another man?"

"Sure." He shrugged. "But I've no interest in guy-on-guy action—that doesn't float my boat. I'm talking about the two of us putting all the focus on you, bombarding you with pleasure until you can't take any more."

A shudder of excitement fell down her spine, and heat blossomed in her core. "Sounds good to me. *Very* good, in fact. Ashley? This something you're up for?"

His face said it all. He looked like a puppy being presented with its favourite toy. "Fuck, yeah. It sounds hot." He raked his gaze up and down her body. "*You're* hot. So, er... what happens now?"

Both men looked at her expectantly. Clearly she was the one holding all the cards here. "In terms of the dating thing, I haven't got a bloody clue. Let's figure that out later. But in terms of the threesome," she grinned, "I say there's no time like the present. What do you reckon?"

Nico turned to Ashley. "My room's bigger. And nearer."

Ashley nodded, then held out his hand to Connie. She ditched her empty drink bottle on a nearby occasional table, the men following suit. Then she manoeuvred her way in between the two of them, grabbed each of their hands and, as one, they began walking towards the staff quarters. Anyone who happened across them would have a pretty good idea of what they were up to, but to her surprise, Connie found she no longer cared. The rumour mill seemed to always be working overtime as it was, so why not *really* give them something to talk about? She was fed up of worrying about what other people thought. It was a form of control, and she was determined not to fall into that trap ever again.

As it happened, they didn't come across anyone between the corridor and Nico's room, and by the time they approached his door, the tremble in Connie's legs was nothing to do with her skyscraper heels. *Fuck, this is really happening.* Anticipation sloshed through her veins, and the heat that had blossomed in her core not so long ago had now ignited and was rapidly increasing. It wouldn't take much to fan the flames into an inferno.

Nico let go of her hand so he could retrieve his key and unlock the door. He opened it, leaned in to switch on the light, then stood back to allow Connie to enter first. As she stepped over the threshold, she was painfully aware that something momentous was about to take place, and of the two pairs of male eyes fixed onto her rear view. She looked over her shoulder and flashed them what she hoped was a sexy smile.

Nico closed and locked the door, sending a fresh wave of excitement crashing through her.

"Back in a mo," she said, then headed for the bathroom, once again feeling their eyes on her.

Behind the closed door, she took a moment to use the toilet, wash her hands, then do a quick check of her hair and makeup. Stupid, really, since they'd be messed up pretty soon anyway. She smiled nervously at her reflection—just because she wanted this, just because the mere idea of it made her want to melt into a puddle of lust, didn't mean she wasn't petrified. The last man to see her naked—no, she wasn't even going to allow him headspace. He wasn't worthy of it.

After giving her hair a quick smooth and her dress a tweak or two, she was ready. Taking a deep breath, she returned to Nico's bedroom. The curtains had been drawn, the overhead light switched off, and only a bedside lamp illuminated the space. Despite the dimmer light, the concern on both their faces as they watched her exit the bathroom was apparent. "Everything all right?" Nico asked softly.

"Yes, thank you," she replied, smiling.

"You sure?" Ashley put in.

"Yes." She knew what he was really asking was—*are you sure about this?* In lieu of a reply, she strode over to the double bed—it seemed longer-serving staff got the bigger, better rooms—sat on its edge and removed her shoes. Then, her fingers trembling slightly, she retrieved the condoms Lisa had stuffed in her bag and held them up with a grin. "I think we'll be needing these, don't you?"

This time the glance the two men exchanged was uncertain. They didn't know how this was going to work any more than she did, which actually made her feel a little better. A thought occurred to her. "Are *you two* sure about this?"

"Yes!" came the instant two-tone reply.

She put the clutch bag on the floor next to the shoes, then shuffled back onto the bed until she was in the centre. Tossing the condoms onto the bedside table, she said, "So what the hell are you waiting for?"

A thrill of power zipped through her as Nico and Ashley leapt into action, toeing off their smart shoes and emptying their pockets before joining her on the bed, one on each side. Immediately, her olfactory sense was assaulted by the scents of hot bodies, cologne, shampoo, and shower gel. It merely added to the sublime sensation of being sandwiched between them, and she could only imagine how much better it would be when they were all naked, skin to skin. Hopefully she wouldn't have to imagine for long.

She reached out and put her hands on their nearest thighs. It felt like an act of possession, somehow. Like she was claiming them. She supposed she was, in a way. Tilting her head to look at Nico, she said, "Kiss me, birthday boy."

He obliged without even a second's hesitation, cupping her face in both hands and capturing her mouth in a kiss that went from zero to horny in the space of a heartbeat. Ashley's thigh tensed beneath her hand, and she squeezed it. Not wanting him to feel left out, she groped around for one of *his* hands. Finding one, she guided it to her thigh, then pushed it higher, hoping he'd get the hint. She didn't want this experience to be all start-stop and giving instructions—it wouldn't be very sexy.

Fortunately, Ashley *did* get the hint. He caressed her leg, so gently at first it almost tickled, then became rougher, more confident as his fingers slipped beneath the hem of her borrowed dress. The thought *borrowed* gave her pause, and she pulled away from Nico's lips with a gasp. "Sorry, but I should take off this dress. It's not mine, and I don't want to, er, get any marks on it."

Nico released her with a smirk. "Well, I'm hardly going to

stop you, am I?"

Ashley chuckled. "And I'm certainly not. It looks great, but I'm sure it'll look even better when it's off."

"All right, all right," she mock-complained, scooting down the mattress. "I get it, you want me to take the dress off. Why don't you take the opportunity to lose some of *your* clothes, huh? Seems only fair."

Within a couple of minutes all three of them had divested themselves of their clothes, which now lay scattered across the carpet. "I..." Connie hardly knew where to look. She wished she had two pairs of eyes so she could more easily drink in the sight of the two gorgeous men. *Naked* gorgeous men. "Could you... get back on the bed, and I'll join you in a second?" So much for not wanting to give instructions, but she knew once they carried on with what they'd been doing, they'd quickly get so lost in lust that there'd be no time to enjoy the sights along the way. She at least wanted to get a quick look at the goods she was soon to sample.

They did as she asked, leaving a gap plenty big enough for her between them. She bit her lip to stop herself grinning when she saw them steadfastly avoiding looking at each other—or each other's cocks, anyway. Both were rock-hard and raring to go. Already she felt spoilt for choice—where to start? For just a moment, though, she wanted to just *look*. To enjoy and admire the contrasts between their bodies. It was clear they were taking the time to check her out, too, so fair was fair.

Even fully clothed, the fact Nico was thicker set was apparent. But now, bare as the day he was born, she could also see he was hairier, more muscular. His long, thick cock thrust proudly from a thatch of black, wiry curls, and was red-tipped and engorged. She gulped, barely resisting the temptation to scurry over and sink onto it. There was plenty of time for that.

After treating him to a lascivious smile, she turned her attention to Ashley. Taller, fairer of hair and skin, slimmer. But no less gorgeous. He was finely muscled, like an athlete. To her surprise, his cock was just as wide as Nico's, but maybe a little longer. Though that could be an illusion, since his pubic hair was cropped close to his body. Either way, they would both certainly do the job.

A trickle of juices seeped from her pussy and wet her inner thighs. She squeezed her legs together in an attempt to quell the sudden ache in her clit. After a couple more seconds of committing this parallel-universe image to memory, Connie hurried to retake her place as the filling in a very sexy sandwich.

This time, Ashley leaned in for a kiss, which she welcomed. She slotted her hands into his dark-blond hair and gripped it, before using it as leverage to pull him harder onto her, deepening the kiss. As their tongues clashed, she felt Nico scoot up closer behind her, finding a way to get in on the action without interrupting what she and Ashley were doing. His soft hair tickled the nape of her neck and upper back as he pressed kisses to the top of her spine, her shoulder blades, leaving delicious tingles in his wake.

At the same time, he crept a hand between her legs and sought her pussy. He drew a finger up through her seam, gathering juices and slicking them over her clit. She groaned into Ashley's mouth as seemingly millions of nerve endings were being stimulated at once, by two mouths and one hand.

After a second, though, another hand—Ashley's, she suspected, given the angle—joined the fray, cupping one of her breasts. The already stiff nipple peaked further beneath his touch, thrusting itself into his palm, begging for attention. God, was it even possible to feel this much pleasure at once? Or would she overload, like an electrical circuit, her fuse blowing and throwing everything off? She hoped not—there was so much more pleasure to come, she was sure of it.

She lowered herself to the mattress, using her grip on Ashley's hair to guide him onto the pillows along with her, not breaking the kiss for even a second. To their credit, both men went with the flow, pausing only momentarily to rearrange themselves before continuing to toy with her tits and pussy respectively. Ashley had switched nipples now, and dared a rough pinch of the nub of flesh, causing her to gasp against his mouth, then retaliate by biting his lip.

He pulled away with a bark of laughter. "Wildcat."

"You started it." She gave him another quick kiss, then released him and turned to Nico with a smile. "Since it's your birthday, you get to choose: top or tail?" She hadn't realised until that moment she was going to take them both at once, rather than one at a time, but now she thought about it, it was obvious. And really. Fucking. Sexy.

He blinked as his lust-fogged brain worked out what she was talking about, then replied, "Tail. And…"

She raised her eyebrows. "And what?"

He grinned cheekily. "Since it's my birthday, can I choose the position, too?"

"I don't see why not. What do you have in mind?" She hoped it wasn't something massively complicated or acrobatic.

"Doggy style. So I can see your gorgeous arse, see my cock disappearing inside you." He bit his lip, the mere description of the act clearly getting to him.

It had got to her, too. In lieu of a reply, she tapped Ashley's leg and pointed to the top end of the bed. With that, all three of them leapt into action. Connie and Nico moved, allowing Ashley room to position himself with his back against the pillows, his legs spread. Connie crawled between them and took his cock in her hand. "Fucking hell," he said, his eyes wide as he stared at her breasts, hanging heavily beneath her. "You're so fucking sexy, Connie, d'you know that?"

"Likewise," she purred, lightly stroking his erection. "You have a gorgeous cock, and I can't wait to find out what it tastes like, what it feels like in my mouth."

He groaned and jerked his hips so his cock thrust roughly into her hand. "Me either. *Fuck,*" he said as she gripped him harder, stroked him a little faster. She wanted him to stay hard, but not get too close to climax. Not yet, anyway.

Just then, she felt the mattress directly behind her dip, and a pair of large, warm hands landed on her buttocks. "I could look at this view forever," Nico growled, giving her arse a hearty squeeze.

Connie gasped, then pushed back against him. "You'd better

bloody not. I need to come, and if you're content to just *look,* then I'm sure your friend here will oblige me." She continued teasing Ashley as she spoke.

"There'll be no need for that," he grumbled. "I'd be delighted to make you come... all over my cock." He rubbed the thick wedge of flesh over her buttocks, no doubt his way of reassuring her he'd put on a condom. The feel of the latex was unmistakeable on her skin.

"Then what are you waiting for?"

Nico chuckled, then there was the brush of knuckles against her crack as he took himself in hand and manoeuvred into position. The broad head of his cock slipped through her labia, then entered her, finding minimal resistance since she was so wet. So fucking *horny.* Two utterly gorgeous blokes, eager to please her? It felt like it should be her birthday, too.

Gripping her hips, Nico exhaled loudly as he sunk, inch by inch, into her. "Fucking hell, Connie. Your pussy is like heaven."

She smiled, despite knowing he couldn't see her face. He felt pretty damn amazing, too, but with two egos held in the palms of her hands—literally in one case—it was probably better to keep quiet. Lifting her gaze to meet Ashley's, she licked her lips teasingly, then held eye contact as she opened her mouth and took him inside. Almost immediately, the salt taste of him hit her taste buds, and she hummed with pleasure before sinking further onto his shaft.

In the meantime, Nico had buried himself balls-deep. Now, with his body pressed up against her backside, and Ashley's glans flirting with her gag reflex, she was quite literally full of cock. It was sublime, heady. As well as the physical sensations, she felt powerful, controlling the pleasure of two men as she was. It could easily become addictive.

Having paused for a moment to gather herself, she began to suck Ashley in earnest, letting plenty of saliva coat his cock to ease her passage as she bobbed up and down. He let out a strangled moan and cupped the sides of her head.

The sound must have kicked Nico into action, because he pulled almost all the way out of Connie's pussy, then shunted back in. Repeated the action, again and again, at a maddeningly slow pace, which nevertheless fanned the flames of Connie's desire. The stretch and thrust of Nico's shaft sparked off all the nerve endings inside her, and her clit burned with the need to be touched.

She moaned, setting off a chain reaction as the sound vibrated up Ashley's cock. "Uhhh, Connie," he said, curling his fingers slightly and digging them into her scalp. "That's so good."

Unwilling to stop sucking Ashley's dick in order to voice her needs, she reached between her legs to take care of it herself. As soon as Nico realised what she was doing, however, he grabbed her wrist and yanked her hand away. "Uh-uh. *I'll* do that."

Hoping he would do it *well,* she placed her hand back on the bed and used it to brace herself as the three of them settled into a rhythm: the forward momentum produced by Nico thrusting into her shoved her onto Ashley's cock, and she was soon rocking back and forth, back and forth, tumbling further and further into bliss. Before long the finer details blurred: she was just one big ball of pleasure, moving ever more frantically until she became vaguely aware of sparks of pain dancing across her scalp as Ashley swore, his cock twitching repeatedly he ejaculated.

As she swallowed, then allowed Ashley's softening shaft to slip from her lips, Nico began to fuck her so fast, so hard, that he struggled to keep his fingers pressed to her slippery, swollen clit. Fortunately, the friction, although without finesse, was so rapid, so furious that when Nico froze and was taken over by climax, she followed soon after. Her core clenched and released, milking Nico's shaft as pleasure overwhelmed her. Their cries mingled, punctuated by gasps and exclamations, until finally, they were done.

Gingerly, Nico disentangled from her and was gone, presumably to ditch the condom. Breathing heavily, she and Ashley repositioned themselves on the bed so that when Nico came back he could snuggle up on the other side of her. Ashley tucked her up against him and pressed a kiss to her hair. "That was amazing, Connie. I've never seen something so erotic in my entire life. You sucking me, your tits swinging, your arse in the air, the noises you made, the pleasure on your face… fuck, I'm getting hard just thinking about it."

She chuckled. "Steady on. I'm all for going again, but give it five minutes, would you?"

"Eh? What's this about five minutes?" came Nico's voice as he curled up behind her.

"Ashley's getting hard again already," she replied, then sighed happily as Nico flung his arm over her waist. "I said I'm all for another round, but to give it five minutes."

"Fuck, you're up for going again? It really *must* be my

birthday!"

Chapter Fourteen

Three days later

Gritting her teeth in an attempt to keep her nerve, Connie opened the gate leading into Will's "domain" as he'd called it. She strained her ears for any sounds of life. Nothing. *Damn it. Where is he?* She wore her walking boots, so if she had to go traipsing all over the estate looking for him, she could and would, but it'd be really nice if she could get lucky and find him right away.

She crossed over to the large shed, heat rising up her neck and face as she recalled what had happened the last time she was here. Not to mention what had happened since with Nico and Ashley—multiple times. At the rate they were going, they'd have to stop raiding the housekeeping department's condom stash, or Isla would smell a rat.

Pushing the lascivious thoughts out of her head, she stood on tiptoes to peer through the shed window. *Thank God for that.* Will sat at his desk, head bent over some paperwork. It was probably boring—wasn't all paperwork boring?—so hopefully he'd be grateful for the interruption. She sidestepped over to the door, and knocked.

"Come in," came Will's surprised response.

Taking a deep breath, Connie opened the door and walked in, then closed the door behind her. She doubted anyone else was around, but she didn't want to risk their conversation being overheard. "Hi, Will."

Will turned from where he'd been marking something onto what looked like a map of the gardens. "Hello, lass." His expression was inscrutable. Was that an improvement on annoyed, or not? She couldn't be sure. "What can I do for ye?"

She shuffled her feet, glanced off to one side, then made herself look back at Will. "The other day, you told me to give you a few days to get your head straight, and then maybe we could continue the tour. So I did. And now here I am."

He raised an eyebrow and huffed out a laugh. "Aye. Here ye are." He regarded her for a moment, then said, "Ye look brighter. On account o' them lads ye've been spending time with, I'd wager."

Connie's heart raced. *Fuck—he knows already!* She'd planned to tell him, rather than him hearing it from someone else, but apparently she was too late. She narrowed her eyes, regarding him right back. Was he pissed off? Amused? Indifferent? She simply couldn't tell just by looking at him, so she'd have to find out for herself. "That's why I've come to see you."

"To tell me ye've been bonking a waiter and a porter? That's none o' my business, lass. Yer a grown woman, they're grown men." He shrugged.

Trying hard not to laugh at his choice of words—who the hell said bonking these days, anyway?—Connie replied, "Not just to tell you, but to explain."

"Like I said, none o' my business. Ye don't need to explain to me."

"Just *listen,* will you?" she snapped, then continued before he got chance to respond. "A lot has happened since we… you know… the other day. I've done a lot of thinking, a lot of soul searching. I've talked it out with a friend. And I had a bit of an epiphany. You see, when I ran out on you the other day, I was scared of romantic entanglements, of getting heavily involved with someone. Of getting hurt. In the process, I know I probably hurt *you*, and I'm truly sorry for that. But my friend helped me realise there was another way to be involved without being... romantic."

Will's eyebrows drew together, and he scratched at his beard. "What are ye talking about? I'm sorry, lass, but yer not making a wee bit of sense. Can ye not just state it plain?"

Could she? She thought for a moment, then decided that yes, she could. In fact, the plainer, the better. She'd give it to him so straight that his answer could only be a simple yes or no. Excellent. Now all she had to do was get the words out of her mouth, which had gone drier than the Sahara, unlike her palms, which were damp. She swallowed. "Yes, all right. I'm dating Nico *and* Ashley. And I'd like to date you too, if you're up for it."

"Date?" Will screwed up his nose. "I'm guessing yer not talking about fancy dinners and trips to the theatre?"

She snorted. "I wouldn't be *averse* to that, but no, what I mean is I'd like to see all three of you on a non-exclusive basis. You know, casual. Nico and Ashley are happy with the situation, and they're aware I'd like to be with you, too. If you'll have me."

He tilted his head to one side. "Yer a unique sort of a lass, ye know that? Doolally, actually, if ye ask me. Most women complain about *one* man driving them crazy, and ye seem to think it's a good idea to have *three* of us on the go."

"So, is that a yes?" She raised her eyebrows hopefully, her pulse racing.

"It's no' something I've ever considered before, but based on what ye've told me about yer past, I understand yer reluctance to get in too deep." He shrugged. "As long as yer no' wanting me to be having some kind o' kinky sex wi' the three o' ye, I'm all fer it. Yer a great lass, Connie, and I'd be honoured to be one o' yer... men. Dates. Whatever ye want to call it."

She took a second to absorb his words, to be sure he hadn't actually told her to bugger off and never darken his door again. Concluding he hadn't, she practically ran over to him and launched herself onto his lap.

"Eh, steady on, lass. I'm no' sure this chair's built for two." Despite his words, he was grinning, and he wrapped his arms around her back, securing her in place.

Connie grabbed his face and planted a kiss on his lips. Then, when he groaned and tightened his arms around her, she kissed him again, but this time it was no peck. She closed her eyes and threw herself wholeheartedly into it, savouring his warmth, the scrape of his beard, the earthy, masculine scent she'd come to associate with him. As lust took over, she allowed it full control.

Already the heat and throbbing in her pussy was such that she couldn't resist grinding against him as they kissed. She was gratified to find him hard beneath her. He grunted and thrust his tongue between her lips, possessing her mouth the way he probably wanted to possess her pussy. Juices seeped from her core at the thought. The condom she'd tucked into the back pocket of her trousers before she'd left to find Will had been incredibly presumptuous, but hopefully she'd soon be glad of it.

The sounds of snatched breaths, groans and grunts swelled around them as their passion ratcheted up. Will gripped her buttocks and kneaded them roughly, so roughly he'd probably leave bruises. But the sparks of pain, the obvious strength of his need, simply made her hotter. Her pussy felt molten and her clit ached. Grinding against Will was no longer enough—she needed him inside her. Now.

Just as she pulled away from their kiss, there was an almighty bang. Connie squealed and almost fell off Will's lap—but luckily he caught her just in time.

He chuckled. "Dinnae worry, it's just thunder." He nodded towards the window, where the sky had darkened and spots of rain had begun to land on the panes of glass. "'Tis dreich out there, fer sure. Ah well—means ye'll have to stay in here wi' me a bit longer, doesnae it?"

Connie smiled, then reached around and retrieved the condom from her pocket. She held it up in front of him. "I wasn't planning on going anywhere just yet, in any case."

His eyes widened, and he shook his head incredulously. "Ye really are quite something, lass. Unbelievable, really."

She quirked an eyebrow. "So you don't want to, then?"

"What? Are ye mad? O' course I want to. Gimme that, and get yer arse on that desk!"

Connie did as she was told, almost falling off Will's lap again in her haste, then perching on the edge of the desk, her entire body burning with lust as she waited for his next move. She didn't have to wait long.

His eyes dark and heavy-lidded with lust, Will stood and

kicked the chair out of the way, then advanced on her. He held the very corner of the condom packet between his teeth, leaving him with both hands free. "Dinnae move." He made short work of her belt, then the button and zip of her trousers. He yanked them down to her ankles, along with her knickers, before pushing them off one of her legs—no easy task given her bulky boots. She scarcely noticed the cold air hitting her fevered skin as Will straightened, then pushed a hand between her legs and cupped her mound, then squeezed it hard.

She gasped. A glint came to Will's eyes, and he hurriedly undid his own trousers, then released his cock. Connie barely got a glimpse of it before Will took the condom packet from his teeth, opened it, and carefully sheathed himself. But it didn't really matter what it looked like—only how it felt inside her. She could hardly wait to find out.

He looked her in the eyes then, a question in his own. She nodded frantically, and that was it. His signal to go. And *Christ,* did he go. In a series of movements shockingly fast for a man of his stature, he closed the gap between them, grabbed her bare leg and held it over his arm, then aimed his cock at her entrance and forged right on in. She was wet, but still tight, and the burn and stretch as his thick shaft penetrated her was delicious.

There was another crack of thunder, then a long, low rumble. Will paused, lodged deep inside her, and met her eyes. "It's getting wilder out there. Means there'll be nobody in the gardens to hear us."

Connie smiled and braced her hands on the desk, hardly

giving its seemingly flimsy nature a second thought. "Fuck me now, Will, with everything you've got. I don't give a shit if the desk collapses."

The laugh he let loose vibrated through her body, and she clenched her pussy in response. Will hissed, then growled. "Ye wee hussy, ye'll pay for tha'."

"Good," she purred, squeezing her internal walls again.

He shoved her flat on the desk and covered her with his big body. Then he proceeded to pound her, the movements fast and furious. God, he was like a machine. She threw back her head and cried out, over and over, as pleasure sucked her up into a vortex, chewed her up and spat her out again. Climax took her in its grip, and her cries morphed into wails as bliss permeated through her entire body, and her core spasmed around Will's cock. "Fuck! Oh fuuuck! Harder! Please!"

He didn't respond, merely reached up and grabbed the other edge of the desk with one hand, using it as leverage as he rammed himself into her. She'd never had sex so primal, so rough, before, and she *loved* it.

As another orgasm slammed into her, taking her breath away, Will froze. Then he gave one, two, three slow pumps before letting out a sound of pure abandon that made all the tiny hairs on her body stand on end. His cock throbbed inside her, releasing its load, setting off further sparks of pleasure that made her gasp.

His eyes closed, Will breathed heavily, murmuring nonsense as he came back down to earth. Then he shook his head and opened his eyes to gaze at her.

"*Wow.*" He tucked a stray strand of hair behind her ear and gave a lopsided smile. The gesture was so tender, so heartfelt, that a rush of affection for him punched her right in the gut. Her stomach flipped as a thought occurred to her: *this isn't going to stay casual indefinitely—with any of them. You might not want to get emotionally involved, but you may not have a choice. The heart wants what the heart wants, after all.*

As Will lifted her and took her into his arms, she came to the conclusion she was all right with that. For now, her mind and body were satisfied—*more* than satisfied. And when her tender, bruised heart was finally ready to join in, she'd welcome it with open arms.

***

A note from the author: Thank you so much for reading *Chasing the Chambermaid*. If you enjoyed it, please do tell your friends, family, colleagues, book clubs, and so on. Also, posting a short review on the retailer site you bought the book from would be incredibly helpful and very much appreciated. There are lots of books out there, which makes word of mouth an author's best friend, and also allows us to keep doing what we love doing—writing.

About the Author

Lucy Felthouse is the award-winning author of erotic romance novels *Stately Pleasures* (named in the top 5 of Cliterati.co.uk's 100 Modern Erotic Classics That You've Never Heard Of, and an Amazon bestseller), *Eyes Wide Open* (winner of the Love Romances Café's Best Ménage Book 2015 award, and an Amazon bestseller), *The Persecution of the Wolves, Hiding in Plain Sight* and *The Heiress's Harem* series. Including novels, short stories and novellas, she has over 170 publications to her name. Find out more about her writing at **http://lucyfelthouse.co.uk**, or on **Twitter (http://www.twitter.com/cw1985)** or **Facebook (http://www.facebook.com/lucyfelthousewriter)**. Subscribe to her newsletter here: **http://www.subscribepage.com/lfnewsletter**

If You Enjoyed Chasing the Chambermaid

If you enjoyed *Chasing the Chambermaid*, you may also enjoy the other multiple partner books I've listed below. My full backlist is on **my website (http://lucyfelthouse.co.uk)**.

The Heiress's Harem Box Set

How does a young woman go from being a long-term singleton, to having four gorgeous guys? Find out in The Heiress's Harem box set.

Contains the complete series, all three books for the price of two—Mia's Men, Mia's Wedding, and Mia's Choice.

Book 1, Mia's Men

Mia's world has fallen apart. Then, just when she thinks it can't possibly get any worse, it does.

Mia Harrington's father just lost his brave battle with cancer. Naturally, she's devastated. With her mother long-since dead, and no siblings, Mia has a great deal of responsibility to shoulder. She's also the sole beneficiary of her father's estate. Or so she thinks.

Unbeknownst to Mia, her father made a change to his will. She can still inherit, but only if she marries a suitable man within twelve months. If she doesn't, her vile cousin will get everything. Determined not to lose her beloved childhood home, she resolves to find someone that fits the bill. What she isn't expecting, however, is for that someone to be into sharing women with his best friend. In the meantime, Mia's friendship with the estate gardener has blossomed into so much more.

She can't possibly plan to marry one man, while also being involved with two others …or can she?

Book 2, Mia's Wedding

Planning a wedding is stressful enough, and that's without a harem of gorgeous men to deal with.

Mia Harrington has had a difficult time of it lately—her father's illness and subsequent death, then finding out she must get married if she is to inherit what's rightfully hers. Fortunately, she's tough and resourceful, and has emerged relatively unscathed from this period, as well as finding herself a suitable husband.

However, things are far from simple. Mia might be planning to marry investment banker Elias Pym, but she's also having a relationship with his best friend, Doctor Alex Cartwright, and is in love with her gardener, Thomas Walker. Add to that broken dates, flashy proposals, a sexy Asian tech billionaire, and a nosey housekeeper, and you've got a situation hectic enough to drive even the most capable person to distraction. Can Mia juggle her men, her job, and the wedding arrangements, or is her happily ever after over before it has even begun?

Book 3, Mia's Choice

But what happens *after* the wedding?

The last few months of Mia Harrington's life have been tumultuous, to say the least. Losing her father, the bombshell in his will, followed by her multiple whirlwind romances and subsequent marriage—it's little wonder she's so thrilled to be spending three weeks in a tropical paradise with her four men. Rest, relaxation and a hefty dose of fun is precisely what they all need.

But the unconventional honeymoon isn't all sea, sun, sand, and scorching sex. Back home in England, they have careers, responsibilities, other things that take up their time. Being in each other's pockets on a tiny island is a challenge—but is it one they can rise to? Will this make or break their relationships? And when being away from it all gives them time to think, what impact will that have on the decisions they make about their futures?

More information and buy links (http://books2read.com/heiressboxset).

Stately Pleasures

There are worse things a girl can do to get a boost up the career ladder.

Alice Brown has just landed her dream job as property manager at Davenport Manor, a British stately home. It's only a nine-month contract to cover maternity leave, but it will provide her with the vital experience she needs to progress in her chosen career.

However, her dream job soon threatens to become a nightmare when she discovers her boss, Jeremy Davenport, in a compromising position. Her shock is exacerbated when Jeremy, far from being embarrassed or apologetic about what happened, manipulates the situation until somehow, she's the one in the wrong. He and his best friend, Ethan Hayes, the head of security at Davenport Manor, give her an ultimatum. Faced with the possibility of losing her job and endangering her future prospects, Alice reluctantly agrees to their indecent proposal.

When the dust settles, Alice comes to the conclusion that

playing their kinky games isn't such a bad thing, after all. But what happens when she thinks she's falling for both men?

More information and buy links (http://books2read.com/statelypleasures).

Printed in Poland
by Amazon Fulfillment
Poland Sp. z o.o., Wrocław